"You do...
I've k....

"I've spent three months learning to want you, and I'm here tonight because I couldn't resist you any longer. When you opened the door to me this evening, it was like having my private fantasy come to life!"

The strong hands on Alina's shoulders tightened implacably, and she was hauled against Jared's taut, waiting length.

"Oh!" Her mouth opened on the small cry of surprise and protest. His lips came down on hers, swallowing the tiny sound and going on to plunder further.

Alina's senses whirled as the energy in his kiss pulsated throughout her entire body, bringing it curiously alive. No, it was impossible not to respond, even if the response was a dangerous impulse to match his astonishing challenge....

STEPHANIE JAMES

is a pseudonym for bestselling, award-winning author **Jayne Ann Krentz**. Under various pseudonyms—including Jayne Castle and Amanda Quick—Ms. Krentz has over 22 million copies of her books in print. Her fans admire her versatility as she switches between historical, contemporary and futuristic romances. She attributes a "lifelong addiction to romantic daydreaming" as the chief influence on her writing. With her husband, Frank, she currently resides in the Pacific Northwest.

JAYNE ANN KRENTZ
WRITING AS

Stephanie James

RENAISSANCE MAN

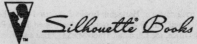

Silhouette Books

Published by Silhouette Books
America's Publisher of Contemporary Romance

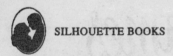

SILHOUETTE BOOKS

ISBN 0-373-80669-8

RENAISSANCE MAN

One

In the end, Alina Corey decided with acute self-disgust, she had made it easy for him. She had surrendered her small fortress without a battle, handed over the keys of the villa, unsuspectingly welcomed the enemy inside the castle walls. In other words, she opened the door of her condominium one cool spring night in Santa Barbara, California, and found Jared Troy standing on the doorstep.

She didn't recognize him, of course. How could she? They had never met except through an exchange of fiery letters begun after Troy had published an article in an obscure little Renaissance studies journal. The battle had been initiated in the letters-to-the-editor column. But when neither had proved sufficiently tolerant to await succeeding issues of the journal in order to wage the newest skirmish, the letters had become direct and even more impassioned. But they had never set eyes on each other. So Alina smiled up at the intent, dark-haired man on the step and wondered vaguely why she felt she knew him even as she realized she'd never seen him before in her life.

"Good evening," she said with a charm she later rued. "You must be Brad Dixon's friend. Won't you come in? You're a little late, but that's all right. There's plenty of food left and the party's just getting into full swing."

For a long, silent second Alina had the sensation of being pinned like a butterfly beneath a pair of nearly green eyes which seemed to flicker with an assessing hunger. The unexpected forcefulness of the man's raking glance sent a faint shiver down Alina's spine. What was the matter with her? she wondered irritably. She was accustomed to the passionate intellectual intensity of some of her academic friends. Hadn't Brad said something about his acquaintance being a poet? Burning glances were de rigueur for poets.

"Thank you," he finally murmured in a deep-timbred voice which fit him perfectly. And then he smiled. There was something very unpoetic about that smile, Alina decided as she politely stepped back to allow him entrance. The slight, mocking twist of his hard mouth had the effect of a small dagger thrust. "It's kind of you to have me in on such short notice."

Alina rallied her uneasy forces, annoyed with herself for succumbing even briefly to her overactive imagination. "No problem," she assured him warmly. "I'm not certain where Brad is at the moment, probably out in the kitchen fixing himself another drink. I believe he said your name was John? I'm Alina Corey. Make yourself at home, John. You know, you really don't look like a poet, although Brad tells me you're a very good one."

He followed her as Alina led the way through a coolly tiled hall and into the uncluttered, almost Mediterranean living room of her home. She had done the entire place in white and rich, chocolate browns, taking pleasure in creating the atmosphere, if not a particularly precise imitation, of a villa by the sea.

Tonight her guests added the glittering contrast of brilliant color and intelligence which made the graceful, restrained surroundings a perfect setting. The living room, with its wall of French glass doors opened to the balmy night and the view of the city and the sea, was crowded with men and women in bright array. The sophisticated, lively crowd of academics, artists and writers had few inhibitions about expressing themselves and their life-style through their clothes.

Alina decided her latest guest added a sober counterpoint to the brightly dressed people around him, and she wondered at the conservative business suit, the dark tie, and the closely trimmed, cocoa-dark hair of Brad's friend, the poet. Still, poets often tended to be a little different....

"What do I look like?" the stranger asked interestedly as Alina led him to a table where several ice buckets held a variety of chilled white wines.

"I beg your pardon?" Alina pulled her hazel glance back from a satisfied perusal of the successful party and smiled inquiringly.

"You said I don't look like a poet," he reminded her calmly, accepting the glass of Chardonnay she handed him. "I was wondering how I do appear to you."

"Oh." Alina narrowed her eyes a fraction and smiled blandly. "Will you be offended if I tell you that you could pass for a prosperous capitalist?"

"A businessman?" His daggerlike smile flashed briefly and he shrugged as he sipped the wine. "Not at all. I understand you're—uh—in trade, yourself."

Alina laughed up at him. "We dealers in books like to think of ourselves as above the common level of commerce."

"Well," he conceded lightly, "if it's any consolation to you, I will admit you don't look like a business woman."

"I'm almost afraid to ask how I do appear," Alina murmured dryly, conscious of a light flush at his appraising expression.

She knew how he looked at her. Poet or not, he *did* have the aura of the quietly ruthless businessman who has made it to the top over a few bodies. A man who looked as if he would be totally professional about the bloodletting along the way. Five hundred years ago, dressed in a suit of armor, this poet could have been mistaken for one of Renaissance Italy's *condottieri,* the soldiers of fortune hired by wealthy city-states to fight the unceasing battles with their neighbors.

The deep-set green eyes were shadowed by surprisingly thick lashes, which lay along the ridge of strong, thrusting cheekbones. The angular line of his jaw had a grim cast that would have looked quite appropriate under an iron helmet. Not a handsome face but one which might have been capable of inspiring more than a little wariness in an opponent.

The extra fillip of experience emanated as an almost tangible force from him. He must have been around thirty-eight, perhaps a year older, Alina decided. The edging of silver at his temples would probably mark the heavy, cocoa-brown pelt of his hair rather heavily in another couple of years.

He was dark and he had an intensity that suggested power, but this poet had none of the sulky, brooding quality she expected from one of his profession.

"You look quite right for the setting you've created," the stranger said quietly. "A modern-day Renaissance hostess, surrounded by a glittering court of dilettantes."

Alina raised a curious, faintly quelling eyebrow. It was all very well for her to relate herself and the world around her to the fifteenth century, but what could this man possibly know of her private passion? Perhaps Brad had mentioned something of her personal interests to him.

"I'll assume that's a compliment," she said dryly, scanning the crowd for Brad. It was about time he appeared to take his poet friend off her hands. Normally it was second nature for her to make a guest feel welcome in her home, but for some reason, tonight Alina was beginning to feel edgy about this poet who didn't look or act like a poet.

"It is," he assured her unsmilingly, studying her once again. "You'd have fit very well into a Medici court. Your hair is a little too brown, perhaps. Not quite the blond ideal of the period, but there's a nicely burnished look to it. In the right light I expect it's almost a tawny color."

Alina's head snapped around as she stared at him, startled by the determined cataloging of her features. It was all she could do to keep from putting a hand to the smooth sweep of light brown hair which she had caught in a deceptively casual swirl at the back of her head. Before she could say anything he was continuing.

"Good eyes," he said with an approving nod as he assessed her slightly slanting hazel glance. "Nice, strong nose. Chin a little on the challenging side but that's all right. A woman of spirit is always preferable to the simpering sort as long as a man is prepared for the occasional battle...."

"John...whatever your name is," Alina began very forcefully, "I don't think..." She didn't need to be told her features were short of the ideal of delicate perfection, especially by a poet whose last name she didn't even know! She had enough self-honesty at the age of thirty to know that her face could most charitably be described as attractively intelligent. But there was no stopping the mysterious John.

"The dress isn't Renaissance style, of course, but the mood is: not-quite-restrained opulence." His gleaming eyes swept the gold-edged cognac silk with its deep purple hem. He even took in the low-heeled, bronze leather shoes with their delicate metallic inserts across the toes.

"I am prepared," Alina stated in an even tone

laced with annoyance, "to permit a certain amount of latitude to the artistic temperament. I am not prepared to tolerate outright rudeness!"

"Naturally not," he agreed at once. "Rudeness has no place in the courtly illusion, does it? Even the direst of challenges must be issued with well-bred civility and wit."

An electric tension lanced across the small space separating them as Alina met the stranger's direct gaze.

"*Are* you issuing a challenge of some sort?" she drawled with a cool humor that only she knew was a trifle forced. Deliberately she tried to make him feel like a minor curiosity. Where was Brad? If he didn't show up soon to take responsibility for his increasingly irksome friend, Alina would hunt him down.

"Not yet. At the moment I'm still assessing the strength of my opponent…"

Before he could finish his startling sentence, the green-eyed man was interrupted by a cheerful, masculine voice.

"Hey, Alina! Have you seen any sign of my friend yet? He should have been here by now. I gave him very explicit directions.…"

Brad Dixon politely shouldered his way through a group of writers vehemently arguing over the merits of the East Coast style of novel. His sandy blond hair and blue eyes were a perfect foil for the dark, royal blue shirt and close-fitting black slacks.

He nodded briefly at the man beside Alina and went on quickly. "He probably got wrapped up in the call of his Muse. Not like him to turn down free food and wine, though!"

Alina's eyes widened as she took in the implications of Brad Dixon's remarks along with his obvious lack of recognition of the stranger at her side. "I was under the impression that your acquaintance had already arrived," she murmured in a chilling little voice.

"I don't see him. You can't miss him when he's around. Full beard, kind of short..." Brad broke off as he realized Alina's assumption. He smiled. "No, this, sure as heck, isn't him! Hello. I'm Brad Dixon. I don't believe we've met. A friend of Alina's?" He stuck out his hand.

"Not yet," the man admitted calmly, ignoring Alina's sizzling look in favor of shaking hands briefly with Brad. "Alina and I are still in the process of getting to know each other. I'm Jared Troy."

"Jared Troy!" Alina sucked in her breath, her fingers tightening dangerously around the stem of her glass. The wave of guilt-inspired panic that washed over her took an incredible amount of willpower to subdue. Jared Troy! And she'd invited him into her house as if he were a welcome guest!

"I'm afraid so," he said half apologetically as Brad excused himself and left in search of the missing poet. Jared eyed her with a trace of what might have passed for amusement. "You didn't give me a chance to introduce myself."

"You made no effort to correct my false impression," she countered icily.

There was no need to panic. He might not know what she had done. He might only have dropped by to meet her since he happened to be in the area. After all, their correspondence had been going on for over three months. Yes, if he were passing through Santa Barbara he might have decided to stop and introduce himself to his feisty opponent.

"It seemed the easiest way to get myself invited inside," Jared acknowledged quietly.

The haunting music of a lute playing a fifteenth-century ballad filtered through the crowded room from the stereo. For an instant Alina felt as if she had been transported back in time. But it wasn't because of the feeling invoked by the lute. Her response was a direct reaction to the probing, speculative and somehow *satisfied* glitter in the green eyes of Jared Troy. He might, indeed, have been a *condottiere* who had just successfully breached the fortress walls without firing a shot.

"Did you think I would have refused to allow you inside my home simply because of our ongoing disagreement?'' she managed with a commendable touch of humor.

''It occurred to me that you might be a little hesitant to continue the discussion face to face,'' he said slowly.

''Nonsense,'' she retorted spiritedly, deciding to take the offensive right from the start. ''Ours is a purely intellectual quarrel. I would hardly have taken such a matter so personally as to bar my opponent from my home!''

''As Battista did to Francesco?'' he murmured, sipping his Chardonnay meditatively.

The names of the Renaissance *condottiere* and the lively, intelligent lady he had wanted were all it took to kindle the fires of battle in Alina's eyes. It was over these two relatively unknown footnotes to history that she had found herself engaged in such passionate battle with Jared Troy.

''That,'' she declared with ringing conviction, ''was hardly an intellectual disagreement! The man had seduced her and then blithely taken his leave! He had a hell of a nerve coming back a year later to try the same stunt all over again! Battista had every right to have the villa doors barred against him!''

''Francesco had a job to do,'' Jared pointed out with suspicious reasonableness.

''Signing a contract to go fight somebody else's

war is hardly the same as catching the eight-o-five commuter train into the city!''

"Battista was a professional courtesan. She knew what she was doing!"

"She was a courtesan because there weren't any other well-paying professions open to intelligent women in those days! Don't equate her with a prostitute. She ran a small palace, had a retinue of servants to feed, responsibilities. Her literary salons were greatly admired, you know. Poets and historians and philosophers came from all over to participate. Your Francesco was damn lucky to even get in the door the first time. She rarely took up with anyone who wasn't as well educated as she was, and Francesco was, after all, merely a member of the *condottieri!*"

"He was good enough to go to bed with her! There is no indication that he resorted to rape! She accepted him as a lover...."

"He seduced her!"

"Battista was the professional seductress!" Jared protested forcibly. His tone was still low but there was an underlying intensity that indicated he was as wrapped up in the argument now as Alina.

"Exactly! And as a professional, she would never have wasted time on anyone who wasn't up to her usual standards unless she had fallen in love. Francesco convinced her that he was in love with her, that he would marry her! He seduced her, dammit!''

"And when he got back a year later he found her with another man.''

"Someone had to pay the rent on the villa and feed all those servants. There is no evidence that Francesco bothered to send home a scudo of his pay!" Alina replied loyally. "He simply showed up a year later expecting everything to be as he left it.''

"Instead of which he was obliged to fight a duel with Battista's current lover!" Jared was all coldly possessive male, as if it had been he himself, rather than a long-forgotten soldier of fortune, who had fought the duel to regain the woman he wanted.

"Typical male approach to the situation. As you may recall, killing off her latest source of revenue didn't exactly endear Francesco to Battista! She still refused to let him into the villa!''

Jared lifted one shoulder in an indifferent shrug and swallowed a third of his glass of wine. "He got inside in the end.''

In spite of herself, Alina smiled up at him with poorly concealed triumph. "You don't know that for certain.''

"Yes, I do. I know Francesco as if he were a close friend....''

"Or as if you were his incarnation?" Alina suggested with acid sweetness.

"You're the one who seems to be having the identification problem," he retorted smoothly, glancing significantly around the gracious, colorful room. "A small change of costume and this could easily be one of Battista's grand literary salons, couldn't it? Loads of bright, witty, well-dressed and well-mannered people busy impressing each other and decorating your living room. How far have you carried the identity mix-up in your own mind, Alina?" The strongly etched lines at the edge of his hard mouth tightened as he scanned the guests.

Alina felt the color wash momentarily out of her face and then return in a vivid wave of red. With great mental effort and a firm reminder of how Battista might have managed the situation, she got control of the hand that itched to slap the intruder's face. Taking a deep, steadying breath, she looked up at him through her lashes, hazel eyes glittering.

"Are you asking me which of the men present is paying my upkeep? Unlike poor Battista, I have other means of earning my living. A few things have changed in the world since her time. I'm not obliged to choose my lovers according to their bank accounts. I do try, however," she concluded in a lofty tone, "to maintain her other high standards of selection."

She could have sworn that a dull flush briefly

marked Jared's tanned cheekbones, but he didn't apologize. Instead he went back on the attack.

"Don't forget that the one time Battista chose a lover without regard for his bank account, she picked Francesco, not one of her effete, scholarly admirers."

"A momentary lapse from which she soon learned her lesson. Francesco did *not* get back inside the villa a year later when he finally saw fit to return for a little R and R!"

"What makes you so sure? There is no record of what finally became of either of them," Jared said with such easy certainty that Alina dared to hope he really didn't know about the business with the microfilmed letters.

"I'm sure of it because I know Battista as well as you think you know Francesco," she said airily. "Battista was too smart to be taken advantage of again by the same man!"

"If he succeeded in convincing her of his love…"

"He got away with it once. He'd never have managed to trick her again. Francesco wasn't in love with her. If he had been, he wouldn't have abandoned her for a year. At the very least, he would have married her before he left on that last campaign and provided for her support."

"There were other factors involved," Jared said mildly. "One didn't casually turn down Medici offers of employment in those days. The least Battista could have done was remain faithful for a year. I'll bet Francesco not only got back inside her villa after he killed her latest lover, I'll bet he took his belt to Battista, too! She deserved it.''

"You obviously have no genuine understanding of the situation," Alina began heatedly, her brows drawing together over her firm nose. "One of these days, I'm going to prove…" She broke off in horror at her runaway tongue. What on earth had possessed her to say that?

"Yes?" he invited politely. "Just what are you going to prove? Better yet, with no known records of their lives other than the ones we've turned up so far, just *how* are you going to prove anything?"

Alina swallowed uncomfortably, searching her brain for a reasonable answer. She was saved from a direct lie by a familiar voice.

"There you are, Alina. I've been looking for you. Someone said you'd disappeared into a corner with a stranger."

Alina gratefully put out a hand to draw the handsome, older man a little closer. It was a small gesture—one she was hardly aware of—but it drew Jared's enigmatic gaze like a magnet.

"Nick, this is Jared Troy. He just showed up on my doorstep. Jared, this is my partner, Nicholas Elden. He's the first half of Elden and Corey Books," she said chattily, anxious to deflect Jared's interest from the subject of why she thought she could find a conclusion to the story of Francesco and Battista.

The two men shook hands gravely. In the soft light, Nick's silvered red head inclined in an almost courtly manner. He was a gentleman, Alina thought, not for the first time. Jared Troy's brusque response stood out in contrast.

"*The* Jared Troy?" Nick was saying in gracious amusement, ignoring the younger man's cool attitude. "The one responsible for sending poor Alina off into periodic rages and vows of merciless vengeance?"

"She does seem to take our little historical disagreement personally, doesn't she?" Jared murmured, his eyes on Alina's annoyed expression.

"That's putting it mildly. I've seen her throw your letters down on the floor and stomp on them when they arrived at the book shop." Nick chuckled.

"Only the ones in which he made particularly inaccurate comments about Battista!" Alina defended herself spiritedly. "I certainly never stomped on the ones which commissioned us to find certain rare books!" she added.

"You two have established quite a reputation for difficult out-of-print and rare-book searches," Jared said in what sounded like an attempt to calm troubled waters. "I was very grateful to Elden and Corey

Books for locating that nineteenth-century history of Renaissance military armor.''

"Alina did all the work on that one," Nick told him with a kindly smile for his partner. "And when it arrived in our shop she went through it very carefully to see if there was any mention of your Francesco before sending it on to you!"

"Afraid I might have accidentally come across some conclusion to the story?" Jared inquired blandly of Alina. "I do have other interests, you know. I haven't devoted my entire life to the tale of Francesco and Battista!"

"No," she agreed cooly, "I didn't think you had. Your interests and collection are well known, Jared. Known and respected."

"Even if my academic background is not?" he prompted with one lifted brow. "It bothers you that I entered your closed little world of the Renaissance via Wall Street instead of from the elite ranks of academia, doesn't it?"

"Of course not!" she protested much too quickly, stung by the appalling accuracy of his comment. She was not a snob. Was she?

"I should hope not." He smiled dangerously. "After all, even the Medici were a family of bankers. The businessmen and the *condottieri*, who were also businessmen in their fashion, made the Italian Renaissance possible."

"Look," Nick Elden interrupted hurriedly, eyeing the flags flying high in Alina's cheeks as she prepared to reenter the fray, "if you'll excuse me, I'll leave the two of you to argue this out. Nice to have met you, Jared. It's been a pleasure having your business over the past few months. I hope we'll get another chance to talk."

The older man removed himself from the tension around the other two, disappearing into the crowd. Alina didn't bother to watch him go, her attention was focused entirely on Jared Troy.

"Your partner, hmmm?" Jared murmured before she could take him up on his earlier statement. "What other role does he play in your life?"

"That's absolutely none of your business," she retorted, sidetracked.

"I'm afraid it is," he countered softly, the green eyes clashing with hers in a way that revived the chill down her spine.

"What are you talking about?" she challenged boldly, reminding herself to stay on the offensive. "Just why are you here tonight?"

"First things first," he replied steadily, still holding her eyes. "I'm here because you more or less invited me."

"That's ridiculous! I've never invited you to my home! Our correspondence has been entirely composed of business matters and our discussion of Francesco and Battista!''

"You invited me, my little virago, the minute you decided to use my name to get hold of a copy of those letters you discovered in the Molina collection.''

The words were casually, almost negligently spoken, but their effect on Alina was electric. She promptly choked on a sip of wine and nearly dropped the glass.

"Are you all right?" Jared asked with what could have passed for genuine concern, she thought uncharitably as she gasped for breath. He pounded helpfully on her back.

"Yes, yes, I'm okay!" she got out, stepping out of the way of his hand before it could descend between her shoulder blades again. "I'll be fine. Just give me a minute. I'll run to the kitchen and get a glass of water...."

"Oh, no, you don't," he murmured mildly, catching hold of a small-boned wrist. 'I'm not coming all this way only to have you slip out the back door on me!''

"I wasn't thinking of doing anything like that!" she objected indignantly, disdaining to struggle against the gentle, but unshakable grip.

He glanced down at the broad, chased gold bracelet on her wrist, rubbing his thumb across the dully gleaming metal with an absently thoughtful gesture. He seemed to be composing his next words carefully before uttering them.

When at last he raised his eyes to meet her wary gaze, there was an intimidating determination in every line of his harshly carved face.

"I suppose," she began carefully, "that you think I should just turn the film over to you? After all the work I did locating those letters and persuading Molina to let them be filmed?"

His mouth quirked upward at her defiantly tilted chin. "Since it was only with the use of my name that you persuaded him to let the letters be filmed, I do have a certain claim on them, don't I?"

Alina ground her teeth against the stupid guilt which again threatened her. So what if she'd had to resort to using his clout to get those letters? She was the one who'd traced them to the Molina collection! She had a right to use them first to write the devastating article which would crush Jared Troy's theories on the outcome of the Francesco-Battista affair!

"You can relax," he advised gently. "I didn't come here tonight to demand the microfilm."

She stared at him uncomprehendingly. "You didn't!"

She'd been prepared for accusations, threats of exposing her rather underhanded methods; at the very least she'd expected him to demand the film as his own.

"I'll admit the business with the film hastened my arrival," he said quietly. "But I was preparing to come to Santa Barbara anyway. The film provided the impetus to make the trip this month instead of next."

"I suppose there's some deep meaning to your statement!"

"Not so deep. I'm only saying I'm here for the same reason Francesco returned to Battista. I've come to claim my lady."

Two

For Alina, the remainder of her lovely, sparkling party passed in a daze. At various points during the evening she told herself she was dealing with an unstable, perhaps actively crazy man. Then she would remind herself of Jared Troy's sober, formidable reputation in the world of rare books. Surely rumors of genuine mental instability would have reached her by now? On such flimsy arguments she talked herself out of calling the police.

Instead, half on instinct, half on sheer determination to maintain the growing reputation of her parties, Alina managed to act as if there was absolutely nothing out of the ordinary about the tall, quiet man who had appeared on her doorstep.

Accustomed to their own eccentricities, which tended to be flamboyant rather than cold and quiet, most of the guests regarded Jared with minor curiosity and general politeness.

Alina lost no time in snagging a white-maned professor of Italian history and smoothly but forcefully introducing him to Jared. Dr. Hopkins was delighted and Alina took the opportunity to escape.

She had reacted in the only way possible to Jared Troy's startling statement, she decided as she hurried off to lose herself in her own crowd. She had blinked in astonishment, her heart skipping a stunned beat as she finally recognized the source of the tingling sensation down her spine. Fear. Pure, primitive, feminine fear. She had never known it before in her life, and already since meeting Jared she had felt its unnerving fingers more than once.

But in the next instant she had recovered herself and her sense of humor. It was all some sort of joke he was playing on her. He was going to exact a bit of revenge for her escapade with the microfilm after all. And the punishment was easy enough to understand. He intended to make her feel a little as the beleaguered Battista must have felt when she had discovered Francesco on her doorstep demanding his rights as a lover.

With a cool nerve that Alina was very proud of, she had smiled brilliantly up into the disturbing green

gaze. "I'm a firm believer in learning from history,"
she had replied in mocking response to his shocking
statement. "I see no reason to repeat the mistake
Battista made."

Fortunately, Dr. Hopkins had appeared at that
point and Alina had succeeded in foisting Jared off
on him.

Her uninvited guest made no further effort to track
her down during the remainder of the evening. He
stood in a corner near an open French door and spent
virtually the entire time talking to the professor of
Italian history. Alina cast him uneasy glances from
time to time as she moved among her guests, but he
seemed oblivious.

It was too much to hope that he would simply walk
out the door with the others when people finally began taking their leave. She slanted a hopeful look in
the direction of the corner he still occupied with Dr.
Hopkins and saw the cocoa-dark head still bent attentively to the conversation he was having with the
older man.

"It's been a great evening, Alina, as usual," Nick
Elden assured her breezily as he trailed Brad Dixon
and the poet, who had finally arrived, out the door.
Brad had been correct about his friend's enjoyment
of free food and wine. The poet had made surprisingly sharp inroads into the refreshments in the short
time he'd been there.

"I'm glad you had a good time," she said warmly, lifting her face for his brief farewell salute.

It was as Nick raised his head with a small show of reluctance that Alina finally saw Jared glance across the room. She knew he'd seen the casual little kiss and she saw the sardonic expression in his eyes as he acknowledged the implications. No harm in letting him know that she was on excellent terms with a number of men, she told herself smugly. Just in case he really did have any notions of carrying out his threats!

"I'll see you at the shop on Monday," Nick was saying pleasantly. "Have a good weekend, Alina."

"You, too." She smiled and watched him leave with a trace of reluctance. The only ones left in the room now were Dr. Hopkins and Jared. She turned just as the professor reluctantly ambled across the thick brown-and-white-striped area rug in front of the white fireplace, aiming toward the door. Jared strode by his side. The two were still deep in conversation.

"The old style of warfare changed completely after the Battle of Marignano in 1515, of course," Hopkins was saying a little sadly as if regretting the change. "With the development of heavy artillery... But I can see it's time to stop talking about guns. Alina, my dear, I'm sorry to be the last one out the door." He, as had most of the other men in the crowd, bent to drop a gallant little kiss on her cheek.

"Not quite the last one, sir." She smiled meaningfully over his shoulder at a blandly watching Jared.

Hopkins looked surprised. "Oh? I was under the impression... Well, never mind. I'll be seeing you soon, I expect, Alina. I can't stay away from your shop long, you know that. It's like an addiction! Jared, it was a pleasure meeting you. I'd like to continue the conversation sometime in the future."

"I'll look forward to it," Jared said politely, waiting silently as the older man disappeared down the steps. "You needn't bother holding the door open any longer for me," he finally advised Alina. "I'm not going anywhere just yet."

With a stifled groan, Alina closed the door and trailed him back into the now quiet living room. She threw herself down onto the curved, white-upholstered banquette, her cognac and purple sheath moving fluidly over the supple curves of her body. Intent on dominating the scene with her only weapon, casual self-confidence, she stretched her arms out on either side of herself along the curving back of the banquette. Crossing her legs with graceful nonchalance, she tipped back her head and smiled aloofly at the man who was watching so intently.

The tiny lines around the corners of his eyes crinkled in wry amusement. "Very nice," he approved, moving to stand beside the fireplace. In deference to the balmy evening, Alina had filled the dark interior of the hearth with dozens of candles in all shapes and sizes. Their cheerfully flickering light had cast a glow over the party without providing unwanted heat.

"Me or the fireplace?" she asked in amusement.

"Both. You do have more than a touch of the style Battista must have had," he said quietly, his eyes on the candles in the fireplace. "But, then, I already knew that." He glanced up, pinning her with his gaze. "I never threw your letters on the floor and stomped on them." He grinned.

Alina made a dismissing movement with one hand. "Nick was exaggerating. I didn't resort to that sort of temper tantrum, either!"

"Liar." He chuckled. "I'll bet he was telling the truth or very near it. I know a great deal about you after all the correspondence we've exchanged. I'm well aware of your spirited feelings on the subject of Francesco and Battista. You defended the lady with wit and style and passion. Just as she would have defended herself. Just," he clarified, "as you would defend yourself, if need be."

"Fortunately," Alina stated flatly, "there is no need."

"I hoped you'd see things that way, but to tell you the truth, I really didn't expect such a reasonable attitude." He rested one arm on the brown tile mantel and eyed her with the same hungry, assessing glance he'd given her when she'd first opened the door.

"I can afford to be very reasonable about a subject in which I'm not particularly interested," she shot back smoothly, her toes curling tensely inside her shoes. She schooled her nerves not to betray any more visible indication of her heightening tension.

"I see." He nodded. "Well, I shall just have to make you take some sort of interest then, won't I? I meant what I said, Alina Corey. You've been seducing me with your passionate, intriguing letters for over three months. I knew, sooner or later, I would have to come and find you. The coup you pulled off by obtaining a copy of that undiscovered material from Molina was the last straw. I couldn't wait any longer. I had to come and see for myself if the real woman was anything like I imagined her from the evidence of her correspondence."

"But I never meant anything…anything personal in those letters!" Alina snapped, taken aback by the sheer satisfaction radiating from him. "I never discussed anything aside from business or the argument we were having over Francesco and Battista! You must know that!"

"It wasn't what you said in your letters so much as how you said it." He smiled. "I couldn't resist. I had to come looking for you, and I wasn't at all disappointed. The real woman is even more intrigu-

ing than the passionate little creature who emerged
from the letters.''

"That's crazy!'' she exclaimed, trying to remain
cool and aloofly amused by the incredible situation.
But she didn't know how long she would be able to
maintain the pose. Already she could feel her nerves
fraying around the edges under the impact of the
electric tension in the room.

He shook his head, stalking slowly over to a brown
leather chair and lowering himself into it with masculine grace. Alina realized with a start that he was
a physically powerful man. He wasn't massive or
bulky. It was a catlike power of lean, coiled strength,
and it was somehow more intimidating to her feminine senses than bulging muscles might have been.

"It's not crazy,'' he countered gently. "I never
discussed anything in my letters to you except the
same subjects, but I'll bet you can tell me a lot about
myself.''

"I've never been tempted to psychoanalyze you
from your correspondence!''

"Try it,'' he invited.

"I'm not sufficiently interested to bother!''

"Did I sound that dull?'' He sighed regretfully.

"Dull!'' she echoed without thinking. "Dull is the
last word I would have...''

"See? You did have some mental image of me,
didn't you?''

She glared at him, one bronze-toed shoe swinging gently in annoyance. "All right," she agreed, goaded. "I'll tell you exactly how I pictured you!"

"I have a feeling I'm going to regret having asked," he groaned ruefully.

"Probably," she told him unsympathetically. She lifted her eyes to the white ceiling with its brown molding and began to tick off her various impressions as if summarizing a job candidate's résumé. "If asked, I would have said you were probably in your forties...."

"Close enough." He sighed wryly. "I'll be forty next year."

"A quiet, self-contained individual, who didn't care for parties such as the one I gave here tonight..."

"Most socializing is a nuisance."

"I would have described you as rather hard and ruthless in some ways," she went on deliberately.

"Why do you say that?" he asked, looking mildly offended.

"That assessment was based originally on your reputation, not your correspondence," she admitted. "Everyone in the book world knows you made your money the rough way on Wall Street and that you still appear occasionally to terrify the market before disappearing into the sunset with a new bundle of cash. There was nothing in your letters to me to

cause me to discount that initial impression. You
were always so ruthlessly logical in your justification
of Francesco's military actions as well as the business affairs of the time. Except, of course," she
amended with a superior smile, "when it came to
poor Battista's business affairs. There was no logic
to the way you criticized her. But you were every bit
as hard and ruthless in your remarks as Francesco
seems to have been!"

"Probably because I'd feel as strongly as he did
about the seemingly endless supply of men she found
to fill those literary salons of hers!"

"She certainly didn't sleep with everyone who
came to the salons! A good portion of her income
came from the admission fees, and those attending
expected and received nothing more than a fine intellectual afternoon or evening. She only took as lovers the pick of the lot! That was the way all the grand
courtesans operated. They were queens of society!"

"We seem to be straying from the subject," Jared
interposed mildly.

Alina's eyes narrowed. "As far as I'm concerned,
discussing Francesco and discussing you are one and
the same exercise!"

"Ah!" There was a wealth of understanding in the
single utterance.

Alina winced as she realized how much of her
image of him she had revealed. "It was only natural

I should come to see you very much as I saw Francesco. I mean, you always argued his case as if you were he!"

"Go on," he coaxed quite gently, a smile in his eyes. "Tell me exactly how you see Francesco and me."

"There's not much more to tell, is there? Quiet, hard, ruthless, interested in making money through the most pragmatic means available; as a *condottiere* in his case, as a Wall Street tycoon in yours." She broke off reflectively, remembering all the other impressions she had garnered from the letters. "We may never know how Francesco invested the money he must have received from his Medici employers, but the odds are he did the same as you and put it into art or rare books. It was common practice then, as now, for men to use such things as a safeguard against inflation."

"Quiet, hard, ruthless," he repeated thoughtfully, turning the words over on his tongue. "Anything else?"

She hesitated, not wanting to reveal what little remained. The last impression had been too fleeting, too intangible, and not very important, anyway.

"Tell me," he murmured, leaning back in the chair and stretching his expensively clad legs out in front of him.

"It's nothing… Probably highly inaccurate!" she muttered.

"Please?"

She wondered at the gentle insistence. "Well, if you must know, I had the feeling you were a little…isolated," she finally said quietly.

"Lonely?" he guessed, using the more accurate term.

"Perhaps." She looked out toward the darkened garden beyond the French doors.

"Is that why you maintained the correspondence?" he asked a little abruptly. She heard the probing need to know. "Because you felt sorry for me?"

"No," Alina replied quite honestly. "I figured that if you were lonely it was from choice. I didn't continue to write to you out of sympathy! I wrote because you were so damn stubborn about admitting Francesco was a bastard!"

He laughed and Alina heard the echo of released tension in the sound. As if her answer had pleased him. "Does it occur to you that we seem to have taken a lot of other things for granted about each other?" He leaned forward, resting his elbows on his knees, clasping his hands loosely.

"Such as?" she demanded haughtily, irked at having let the conversation become so personal but unsure how to stop it. He *did* have a legitimate reason for being here after what she'd done by misrepresenting him to Molina.

"You knew I wasn't married, didn't you?" he asked shrewdly.

She blinked and then nodded slowly. "I guessed you weren't."

"Just as I knew you weren't. There was too much energy and passion in the letters. Did you realize that?" he asked wistfully.

"Nonsense!"

"It's true. I knew from the first that there was no particular man in your life. But knowing Battista, I figured you probably had a whole court of unimportant men hovering around. And I was right about that." He didn't look pleased at the notion.

Alina suddenly grinned, finding his displeasure enormously amusing. "A whole court of unimportant men hovering about is exactly the way I like it!"

He glanced at her sharply. "Because it's safer that way?" he hazarded.

"Because it's much more pleasant than making one man important and having him disillusion you!" she snapped back.

He looked straight at her. "I know what it means to be disillusioned. You're not alone. Why do you think it took me three months to work up the nerve to come and get you?"

"What are you talking about?"

"I was terrified that when I finally came for you, I'd find I'd been wrong in everything I'd learned from those letters," he said as if confessing a grave weakness in himself. "I was afraid you might turn out to be cold or passionately in love with someone else or cruel in the ways only a woman can be cruel." He saw her staring at him in blank astonishment and shook his head wryly. "I mean, I *knew* everything would be all right. Intellectually and, for the most part, emotionally, I was sure of what I would find. But some small part of me was still a little afraid. Don't you understand?"

"No!" Alina yelped, appalled. She rose to her feet in a restless movement, and almost instantly he was standing in front of her. "I do not understand any of this! You show up at my door and get yourself inside by trickery...!"

"A slight misunderstanding on your part," he soothed.

She ignored him. "And then you tell me you know about that business with the microfilm. Then you start sounding as if you'd followed me halfway around the world...."

"Instead of just from Palm Springs?"

"What little humor there ever was in this bizarre situation is gone. I'll thank you to stop teasing me. I don't know what you're after unless you're somehow trying to get that microfilm from me! And I can tell you right now, I'm not going to give it up until I've learned all I can from it. I'm going to prove once and for all what finally happened between Francesco and Battista!''

"I'm not after the film,'' he interrupted gruffly, his hands coming out to close over the thin silk on her shoulders. "I'm after you, can't you get that through your head? I want you, Alina Corey. I've spent three months learning to want you, and I'm here tonight because I couldn't resist you any longer. When you opened the door to me this evening, it was like having one's private fantasy come to life!''

"I'm not Battista!''

"I'm not Francesco!''

"I'm not so sure about that!'' Alina stormed.

She was about to say more, much more, but suddenly it was too late. The strong hands on her shoulders tightened implacably, and she was hauled against the taut, waiting length of him.

"Oh!'' Her mouth opened on the small cry of surprise and protest. His lips came down on hers, swallowing the tiny sound and going on to plunder further.

Stricken with the unexpected impact of the hungry, literally ravishing embrace, Alina stood utterly still, her fingertips braced against the dark fabric of his jacket.

It had all happened too fast, she realized dimly.

He had gone from the verbal argument to the physical one before she had fully realized the depths of her danger.

The force of his desire came at her in waves. The hunger in his kiss was like that of a wild creature which has been pent up far too long. The fundamental need in him poured over her as he explored the warmth of her stunned mouth.

She almost flinched as the tip of his tongue flicked along her lower lip in sharp, urgent little movements. Then it moved further, seeking out her own tongue and drawing it forth into a sensual, intimate battle.

She reacted because there was no option, she told herself. Against such an assault, every instinct rallied to fight back. But the skirmish loosed other powers, powers that involved more and more response.

His hands slid down from her shoulders, his fingers probing through the silk to find the contours of her slender back. "My God!" he murmured huskily, not quite lifting his mouth from hers. "I've dreamed of this for three months. You don't know how I've ached...."

Before she could protest, tell him it was impossible to want a woman so intensely just from three months of correspondence, his mouth was once again moving damply, warmly on hers.

Alina's senses whirled as the energy in his kiss pulsated throughout her entire body, bringing it curiously alive. No, it was impossible not to respond, even if the response was this dangerous impulse to match the challenge in him. In some ways, she knew, it would probably be safer to shrink before it. But something in her would not allow the weakness of such a reaction.

"Alina, my sweet, passionate Alina!" he grated. She felt the fine trembling in his hands as they worked their way down to her waist and then tugged her lower body closer to his own.

She was left in no doubt of his highly aroused state. He forced her thighs gently against the heat of his own, urging her silently to accept the reality of his need.

"Jared, please...!"

"Don't tell me to stop," he pleaded, tracing the line of her jaw with his lips. "I know you too well. You don't really want me to stop, so please, don't say it!"

"You can't know me that well!" She shivered as his teeth sank gently into her earlobe, closing around the tiny, glittering amethyst earring she wore. "Jared! We've only written each other a few letters! Be...be reasonable! We've done nothing but argue...."

"Trust me, sweetheart," he breathed, releasing her ear to bury his face against the nape of her neck. He caught the fine, soft hair there with his lips and gently tugged. The tiny sensation of pain was exquisitely, astonishingly erotic. Alina gasped.

She felt the satisfaction in him as she trembled against him, her eyes shut tightly against the unfamiliar level of her own reaction. What was the matter with her? This wasn't like her! It wasn't how she wanted to be! She had created exactly the world in which she wished to live and this sort of passion had no place in it.

Jared's hands slipped lower, cupping the roundness of her bottom and sinking his fingers luxuriously into the silk-covered flesh.

"You were right, you know," he breathed against her throat, the tip of his tongue tasting her skin. "I have been isolated, lonely...."

"Jared!" She didn't want any masculine appeals to her softer instincts! That was an old trick and she was wise to it.

He lifted his hands slowly along her rib cage until his thumbs rested under the weight of her small breasts. "Don't fight me," he begged, inhaling the scent of her. "I've been wanting you for so long. Wanting your passion, your fire, your warmth..."

"Stop it, please stop it!" she hissed and then swallowed thickly as his thumbs sought the budding tips of her unconfined breasts. "You don't understand!"

"What don't I understand?" he challenged. "I know you so well."

"Damn you, Jared Troy!" she rasped, "I won't let you do this to me! I've found my world, created my own niche in it. You're not going to come along and ruin everything!"

With every ounce of strength at her command, she pushed against the solidity of his chest. She succeeded in forcing a small distance between them, and then his hands went back around her, not pulling her close, but locking her within the confines of a loose embrace. Green eyes flames avidly, longingly over her as she tipped her head up to face him.

"Don't be afraid of me," he murmured as if soothing a frightened young filly. He swayed her gently to and fro in his arms. "There's nothing to be afraid of. It's going to be all right...."

"Will you stop talking to me as if I were an hysterical sheep or something!" Alina exploded. "I'm not afraid of you, I'm simply trying to tell you I'm not interested in an affair with a man I've barely met and with whom I've exchanged nothing but arguments!"

"You knew me well enough to take the risk of using my name to sweet-talk Vittorio Molina into having those documents filmed." He grinned engagingly.

"That's got nothing to do with it! I'd have done just about anything to get hold of a copy of those letters! And if you're suggesting I should be willing to go to bed with you in order to repay you, you're out of your mind!''

"You just said you'd do just about anything to get hold of them...." he taunted lightly, confidently.

"It's much too late to convince me I need to go to bed with you in order to get them. I've already got my hands on them. The first you're going to know of the contents of that film is when I publish my rebuttal in the *Journal of Renaissance Notes and News!*''

"By that time I won't care about your rebuttal. I'll have you safely in my bed.''

She shook her head disdainfully. What was the matter with him? Didn't he know how to take no for an answer? "I meant it, Jared,'' she told him steadily. "You're not going to be allowed to disrupt my life. No man is. I've got everything I want, and there's no room for an affair with you.''

For the first time she saw a flicker of doubt in the green gaze.

"Are you,'' he asked very carefully, "trying to tell me there's someone else?''

"A whole roomful of someone elses,'' she retorted. "Didn't you see that tonight? I get all the masculine attention I need or want, Jared.''

He went very still. "You're not in love with any of the men who were here tonight. I would have known!''

"I love them all." She smiled easily. "And they love me."

"Don't you dare try to tell me you've been to bed with any of them! I'd have known, dammit! Oh, I saw all those charming good-night kisses, but that's all they were. There wasn't a male in the group who's getting any more than a good-night kiss from you!"

"I'll grant you that," she agreed lightly, slipping out of his slackened grip and stepping just out of reach. "And that, too, is precisely the way I want it. Everything in my life is precisely the way I want it. I've worked hard to make it that way."

"And a serious commitment to one man doesn't fit into your gracious, superficial, courtly little world, is that it?" He searched her face so intently that Alina experienced another little shock of guilt. As if she was deliberately demolishing the private fantasy he'd come here tonight hoping to find.

"Serious commitments, as I've learned the hard way, have a habit of dissolving overnight. No, Jared, I'm not looking for a serious commitment. Not anymore. That was a stage I went through in my twenties. I'm over it now."

His face softened as he observed the remoteness in hers. "Tell me about it," he said.

She quirked an eyebrow, stooping gracefully to pick up a couple of empty glasses. Deliberately she

started toward the kitchen, aware that he was following her. "Confession time?" she murmured. "I tell
you about my great disillusionment and you tell me
about yours?"

"Why not? It's as good a place to start talking as
any."

She swung around in the kitchen doorway, and he
nearly collided with her. "You're serious, aren't
you?"

"Very."

Something in him tugged at her, filled her with a
hopeless sense of loss. Which was utterly crazy.
She'd made her decision and she intended to stick to
it. Alina lifted her chin in unconscious defiance. "I
will try to explain this in the simplest possible terms,
Jared. I was married three years ago to a handsome,
charming, brilliant professor of twentieth-century
philosophy. Within the year he had used the incredible rationales available in twentieth-century philosophy to justify sleeping with one of his beautiful,
brilliant students."

"Alina..."

She lifted a hand to ward him off. "Let me finish.
I want you to understand completely. In the painful
months everyone goes through after a divorce, I
stumbled across the story of Battista. I knew what
was waiting for me when I reentered the social
world. Everyone knows what the world of the des-

perate, swinging singles is like. I wanted no part of it, but I also knew myself well enough to realize I'm basically a sociable creature. Battista, I saw almost at once, had solved the problem. She had the world coming to her.''

A slow smile lit Jared's green eyes. "So instead of joining the wild singles' scene, you decided to take a leaf out of Battista's book, is that it? You made the world over in your private Renaissance image.''

"It wasn't hard, but there is a key," she informed him coolly, turning back into the kitchen and depositing the glasses on the counter.

"The key is to convince yourself and therefore everyone else around you that you really don't want to remarry." Alina swiveled around on her heel, bracing herself against the white-tiled counter as she faced him, smiling. "It's a matter of basic male psychology. Men feel 'safe' around a woman who isn't threatening them with marriage or too many demands. In a perverse way they start falling all over themselves to have the butterfly that no one can catch.''

Jared lounged in the doorway, watching her as if she were, indeed, a colorful butterfly he wanted in his net. He said nothing.

"It started out as a kind of game," Alina admitted, thinking back to the traumatic first year after her divorce. "I told myself I would simply follow Battista's rules for handling men. She really took very few as lovers, you know. Battista wasn't a prostitute. She was the quintessential tease, Jared. She gave a man everything but herself. The vast majority enjoyed her charming company, her intellect, her good food, and the brilliant, colorful guests she invited to her parties. But that was all they got."

She paused tauntingly to see if he wanted to argue the point. When he still remained silently propped in her doorway, Alina shrugged lightly and continued.

"As I said, it started out as a game. A way to build a social life without recourse to the singles' bar. I had been a faculty wife long enough to know just what appeals to the intellectual type. I used what I had learned, what Battista had taught me, and I set out to be the perfect incarnation of the kind of lady who could dominate a Renaissance court. It was a challenge," she added with a curving twist of her mouth. "And I intended to do it only until the right man came along. After all, underneath the veneer, I was still Alina Corey who knew she wouldn't be happy unless she remarried."

"When," he asked interestedly, "did you discover you were no longer that Alina Corey? That Battista had, indeed, become a part of you?"

She laughed. "Full marks for you perception," she applauded. "About a year ago, I think. It's difficult to pinpoint the time. It was an evolutionary process. I didn't just wake up one morning and realize that I no longer had any interest in marriage, that my life was too full, too exciting, too interesting as it was. I think I first acknowledged it to myself after I turned down an offer of marriage from a man who was an ideal candidate for Mr. Right. I declined his offer without even pausing to think, and later I realized the old Alina Corey would have jumped at the chance. He was perfect. A successful writer with an interest in history. Good-looking, charming, intelligent and affectionate.''

"And you turned him down without a qualm."

"I'm afraid so," she murmured. "He asked me one evening shortly after I had discovered that Francesco had had the nerve to show up at Battista's door a year after leaving her. All I could think about during the champagne and candlelit dinner Mr. Right was treating me to was getting back home so that I could find out what had happened. I spent the rest of the night pacing up and down my living room in a rage because, when I finally got rid of Mr. Right and got back to my books, I learned there was no record of what had become of Battista and Francesco!''

"You were more wrapped up in their story than in your own, is that it?" He dislodged himself from the door frame and came toward her, a considering look on his strong face. "Or perhaps it would be more accurate to say that Battista's story has become your own story.''

Alina sensed the faint, masculine menace in him and moved lightly out of his path, ostensibly to put the glasses into the dishwasher. "I'm only trying to make it clear to you, Jared, that I am quite happy with my life. I love my books, my parties, my work. I have no need of anything else, especially marriage."

"Who," he asked very casually, "said anything about marriage?"

Three

The glass Alina had been putting into the top rack of the dishwasher slipped from her hand as Jared spoke. She barely caught it before it fell. Slowly she straightened and faced him, a cool fury staining her cheeks and flashing gold sparks in her hazel eyes.

He stood eyeing her with sardonic amusement. The expression replaced the urgent longing which had been radiating from him only a few moments earlier. "You said Battista was the ultimate tease," he drawled, "but she made one mistake in her career, didn't she? Francesco was the one man who demanded and got everything from her. He got more than just the fine food and sparkling company which others paid for and received. He even got more than the lucky few she took to her bed. She fell in love with Francesco, didn't she? And that's why she was so damn mad when he showed up a year later. Any other client who paid his tab would have been welcomed as a repeat customer. But Francesco had claimed everything Battista had to give as a woman and then disappeared. She barred him from the villa when he returned because she was afraid of him...."

"Battista was afraid of no man! She could handle them all!"

"Except Francesco. Her low-born *condottiere*, who had bought his way into the upper classes by selling them his sword, who couldn't even read Latin or Greek, and who collected art as an investment rather than out of noble appreciation, he was the one who reached out and caught the butterfly in his net, wasn't he?"

"Battista learned her lesson." Alina sniffed, slamming the dishwasher shut.

Jared came away from the counter, catching her gently by the shoulders and holding her still in front of him. "Don't try barring me from your home the way Battista tried to do with Francesco. It won't work with me, and I'll lay you odds it didn't work with him. It's too late. You, like Battista, have already given too much of yourself to a man. Oh, yes, it's true, honey. You put all of your inner warmth and passion in those letters you wrote to me. You revealed too much of yourself. Did you think you were somehow safe letting down your barriers with a stranger through the medium of those letters? Or did you have an illusion of safety because you could pretend to yourself that you were discussing another woman's feelings instead of your own?"

"I think," Alina forced herself to say evenly, "that it's time you left!"

He hesitated and then nodded slowly. "I suppose it is. But I'll be back. I know too much about you, and I'm going to use everything I've learned over the past three months to convince you to come to me."

"Why, you arrogant, insufferable...!"

"Careful," he advised with a flash of white teeth, "or I'll demand that microfilm back before you've had a chance to write your scathing rebuttal for the journal!"

"You're not getting your hands on that film until I'm finished with it!" she vowed seethingly.

"How can you deny that I have every right to it?" he inquired with mocking reasonableness.

"I worked hard tracking those letters down! They belong to me!"

"They might have, if you had figured out another way to persuade Molina to film them for you. But you decided my name would be the magic key you needed, didn't you? You knew Molina would be impressed by a request from me…!''

Alina chewed her lip for an instant, anxious to change the topic. ''How did you find out what I'd done?'' she finally asked slowly. ''I just got the film yesterday.''

He slid his hands from her shoulder up to encircle her throat, his eyes warming with private humor. ''I'll tell you in the morning,'' he promised softly, ''over breakfast.''

He used the gentle hold on her throat to keep her still for his kiss. This time he didn't ask for a response. His lips molded hers with quick possessiveness, and then he was freeing her, striding toward the door.

Without a backward glance at Alina's bemused face, Jared let himself out into the night. Belatedly jerking herself free of the enthrallment he had succeeded in placing on her senses, she hurried to the window in time to see a sleek black Ferrari pulling away from the curb. It disappeared down the hill and into the night.

Alina realized with a start that her fingers were shaking as she lowered the white curtain. Almost compulsively she headed toward her study at a quick, light run. It was as if she had to make certain, had to be sure nothing had happened to the precious film.

She swung around the door into the white-carpeted

room, reaching the old oak rolltop desk in a rush. Yanking open the drawer she drew a sigh of satisfied relief at the sight of the little film canister. Of course it was safe. Why shouldn't it be? Jared Troy had been in the living room every moment. And he wouldn't have known where to start looking anyway.

Still, she told herself resolutely, as long as he was anywhere in the vicinity she would have to take care. Slowly she shut the desk drawer. She knew Jared Troy very well after three months of impassioned argument, in spite of her attempt to deny that earlier. He hadn't fooled her for an instant this evening. He'd come to Santa Barbara for one thing and one thing only. He wanted the microfilm she'd wangled from Vittorio Molina's private collection of rare historical books and papers.

Flinging herself down into the leather chair behind the desk, Alina leaned back and propped her crossed ankles on the oak surface. The bronze leather of her small, low-heeled shoes gleamed in the lamplight, throwing sparks off the delicate inset pattern of metallic trim. With a determined frown she studied the portrait on the opposite wall. With the ease of long familiarity she met the eyes of the other woman who shared her study.

It was not a genuine portrait of Battista, of course. Alina had never been lucky enough to find one and couldn't have afforded a genuine Renaissance paint-

ing even if she had found it. The artist had been a
modern one, but he had caught the essence of what
Alina knew Battista must have been—what the new,
emerging Renaissance woman must have been like.

She was dressed in a rich gown of green velvet
and gold brocade. Her near-blond hair was piled high
in one of the elaborate coiffures of the age, a string
of pearls marking the artificially high forehead. Battista, like many fashionable women of the Renaissance, had probably plucked her hair to achieve that
much-admired high forehead. The brocade bodice of
the gown was cut very low, revealing an elegant
curve of breast. Gold and emerald chains encircled
the slender throat. The portrait was cut off at the
waist, but Alina knew the woman would have been
wearing the high-heeled slippers that came into fashion during the time, partly as a defense against
muddy streets, but ultimately because women had
liked the look of them.

The clothes and jewelry were beautiful, a feast for
the eye. But it was the face of the woman that held
the attention. There was no smile on the sensuous
lips. People took portraits seriously in those days.
But Alina was sure there was humor in the blue-
green eyes. Certainly there was a hint of elegant challenge. Battista had forced the world to come to her
on her terms.

''He wants to know what happened to you, Battista," Alina told her friend and mentor. "He's as curious as I am. But he's another Francesco. He thinks he can seduce me into giving him the film. You should have heard him tonight. All that talk of having fallen for me because of my letters. It's just a ruse, naturally. He'd do anything to get hold of the film and prove to himself that he was right about the ending of your story."

She toyed with a pen, thinking of the man who had intruded into her world tonight. Jared Troy had been not quite real to her for the past three months. A safely distant fantasy man from the past. Not one who could ever reach out and put his hands on her. Until this evening.

She shivered for no accountable reason and got restlessly to her feet. The bronze shoes sank deeply into the plush white carpet as she trailed slowly over to the window. Her condominium was perched on a hill above the town. Below her an array of lights washed down to the ocean's edge. The night-darkened Pacific stretched on from there to infinity.

She felt the familiar guilt that always welled up when she remembered how she had used Troy's name to convince Molina to have the documents filmed.

"But he's being just as underhanded in his efforts to get the film from me," she declared staunchly to Battista. "He didn't just show up at my door tonight and demand that I at least share the information with him. He probably knew I'd never surrender it until I have the answers, regardless of how guilty I feel! No, he was much craftier. He thinks he can seduce me the way Francesco seduced you. But I won't make the mistake you did, Battista. Francesco threw a real monkey wrench into your life, didn't he? And then he walked out, leaving you to put all the pieces back together again.''

Alina caught her lower lip between her teeth as she thought about her own past. The divorce had been a traumatic experience. All divorces were. But she knew in her heart that it hadn't been the emotionally damaging experience Battista had been through with her Francesco. Alina had been lucky. It was only after her professor of philosophy had betrayed her that she realized he had never been and never would be the great love of her life.

She'd begun creating her Renaissance fantasy, using all of Battista's cleverness, with the vague notion of somehow finding the great love she thought must be waiting for her. She would know him when he came along, she thought. He would be intelligent, beautifully mannered, witty and utterly captivated by her. So entranced, in fact, that she would never have to wonder if he was out sleeping with one of his students! Because, of course, he would probably be a professor. A successful author or artist had also been a distinct possibility, she acknowledged, but he would definitely be well educated and well acquainted with the elite world of academia. He would most certainly not be a businessman!

And then, after having put together her witty, glittering court of literary and academic friends, it had dawned on her that she no longer needed that great love, that, in fact, it was undoubtedly a mythical thing, anyway. She was, to put it simply, content with the world she had created.

With the perverse manner of the world, that inner satisfaction had somehow only served to attract other people and success in general. She had, Alina told herself once again, everything she wanted. No brash, domineering, arrogant male was going to convince her otherwise.

"Thanks for the chat, Battista." She smiled at the portrait as she swung around to walk out of the room. "Keep an eye on the microfilm for me, will you?"

It was the sound of the doorbell ringing far too early for a Sunday morning which finally roused Alina from sleep several hours later. She pushed the long hair out of her eyes and blinked owlishly at the clock on the white bedstand. Who would have the nerve to be ringing her bell at this hour after a late party?

She waited a few more minutes, hoping whoever

it was would go away, but such luck was not to be
hers. Perhaps it was something important.

Pushing back the bedclothes with a groan, she
fumbled in the closet for a green velvet robe and
belted it around the green satin nightdress she wore.
A glance in the hall mirror as she passed showed a
sleep-tousled woman gowned in a tight-sleeved, low-
necked robe which could have been worn five hundred years ago. It was an incongruous picture, Alina
thought with a wryly twisted smile. The robe looked
much too elegant to be worn with sleep-mussed hair
and no makeup.

"Who is it?" she called, her hand on the door-
knob.

"Jared," came the crisp response. "I've got something for you."

Alina started fully awake, her hand freezing on the
knob. "What on earth are you doing here at this
hour?"

"Open the door and you'll find out." His deep
voice sounded patiently amused. "I told you, I've
got something for you."

With a barely stifled sigh, she opened the door a
crack, peering out resentfully. "No," she said flatly.

"No, what?" he asked innocently.

"No, you aren't getting your hands on my microfilm."

He looked very wide awake, she thought broodingly and wondered vaguely where he'd spent the night. He was wearing dark slacks and a long-sleeved, pin-striped shirt. The collar was open and the sleeves were rolled up on sinewy forearms. There was a fair amount of very tanned, hair-roughened masculine flesh on display.

"I didn't come here for your microfilm," he assured her with his quick, dagger smile. "I'd much rather get my hands on you—Wait!"

He caught the edge of the door just as she stepped back into the hall and tried to slam it shut. Fast as his reaction was, it wasn't quite quick enough to stop the door in time. In horror, Alina saw it close briefly on his fingers.

"Jared!" she squeaked in dismay, yanking the door quickly open. "Oh, Jared, I'm sorry!"

He said something explicit and unprintable, cradling the injured fingers carefully in his other hand. He shot her a reproachful look from under dark brows.

"Are you...are you all right? I tried to stop it before it closed completely. Do you think anything's broken?" Seriously concerned, Alina reached for his hand. He gave it to her with alacrity, the rest of his body following smoothly across the threshold. "They don't appear to be bruised," she said, not noticing he was inside the hall until he closed the door softly behind him.

"They're fine." He chuckled, withdrawing his hand. "There was a good sixteenth of an inch to spare. Close, but no prise, I'm afraid."

She glared at him. "Do you always get inside people's homes with tricks?"

"Believe it or not, I occasionally get an invitation. Stop frowning at me like that. Don't you want to know what I've got for you?"

"A bribe?" she suggested sweetly. "It won't work, you know. You couldn't offer me enough money to make me give up the film."

"Breakfast," he declared succinctly.

"What?"

"I've brought breakfast for you. It's in the car. Go get dressed and we'll take it to the beach."

She eyed him warily. "It's foggy outside. It'll be another couple of hours before it lifts."

"Details, details. Where's your sense of adventure, woman?"

She thought about that. Where *was* her sense of adventure? She could handle this man. She had something he wanted, and she wasn't about to hand it over. It was a contest of sorts. An intriguing game. That was the way to look at it. The man hadn't been born who could defeat both her and Battista. She smiled slowly.

"Yes," he murmured, seeing the smile. "I rather thought you'd see it that way, sooner or later. If I were the truly sporting type, I'd remind you of what happened to Battista after she decided she could handle Francesco...."

"Will you still be looking so pleased with yourself after I've published the ending of their story?" she mocked, turning to walk crisply back down the hall.

"Knowing, as I do, how it will end, I expect I will."

"I'll bet Francesco had that expression on his face when he first knocked on Battista's door after killing her lover in that duel! Shortly before she dropped the contents of the kitchen slop pail on his head from the second-story window!"

"You made that up," he accused. "There's no record of her doing any such thing. Stop embellishing history and go get dressed."

She left him in the living room and walked back to her bedroom with a regal tilt to her head. Carefully she reached out and closed the door of the study as she went past. No sense tempting him to start prowling around in there. She smiled to herself as she caught Battista's eye just before shutting the door, however. Last night she had been taken off guard. This morning she was prepared to deal with Francesco's reincarnation.

She wore the snug-fitting jeans which were really the only practical choice for the beach, but added the touches of which Battista would have approved: a ruffled blue chambray shirt and a cream-colored, shawl-collared jacket of softest chamois trimmed in bold brown stitching. She belted the buttery jacket with a wide silver and turquoise belt and stepped into short, medium-heeled boots. With her shoulder-length hair caught up in a loose twist that left wispy tendrils to tease her throat, she felt rakish and daring.

Jared's green eyes glittered with approval as she reappeared in the living room. "I wonder how the Renaissance poets who spent hours composing odes to a woman's dress or her jewels would have dealt with the advent of jeans." He chuckled.

"If men still wrote poems about women's clothes, perhaps no one would have bothered to invent jeans!"

"It would have been a serious loss to the world," he drawled, taking her arm. "I like you in silk, but there's something challenging about a woman in jeans. Hungry?"

"After all that exercise I had trying to smash your fingers, yes. What did you bring? Better yet, where did you find anything at this hour of the morning?"

"Nothing like a little mystery to arouse a woman's interest," he declared complacently.

"Well?" she demanded as he eased her into the Ferrari.

"I found a bakery," he admitted. "Fresh croissants, unsalted butter and coffee. Will that do?"

"Perfectly."

"I thought it might. Our tastes in many things are quite similar."

"You're so sure of yourself," she marveled, slanting him a sidelong glance as he guided the sleek car down the hill into town and toward the beach.

"During the past three months I've spent a lot of time reading between the lines." He chuckled. He drove with quiet flare. Efficiently, competently, but not recklessly. It was probably the way Francesco had ridden his war-horse.

She heaved a dramatic sigh. "Okay, why don't you tell me how you found out I had the film?"

"Simple enough. Molina called me yesterday morning."

"He called you!" she gasped, flinging herself around in the seat. "He *called* you! Why on earth should he have done that? I deliberately handled the whole thing as a routine request."

"He was curious about why I should be interested in the letters of an eighteenth-century English tourist. He knows my main focus has been on Renaissance military history."

"What...what did you tell him?" Alina whispered, thinking of the jeopardy in which she had placed her professional reputation. If a collector like Vittorio Molina had discovered she'd lied...!

Jared's mouth twisted briefly. "I'll have to admit,

the call took me by surprise. Fortunately, he casually mentioned your name as the dealer who had made the request on my behalf. As soon as I heard that, I was able to put two and two together fairly quickly. I knew there was only one reason you'd risk misrepresentation.''

''Battista and Francesco.'' Alina sat back, a little more relaxed. Apparently he'd covered for her with Molina. The extent of the relief she felt was considerable.

''Right. So I said I wasn't sure yet what I was going to find on the film but that I had hopes of pursuing the history of a particular *condottiere.* I left it pretty vague but he seemed satisfied.''

''And as soon as you hung up the phone, you raced over here to find out exactly what I'd discovered,'' she concluded with a decisive little nod.

''It was, as I told you last night, the last straw. I couldn't wait any longer to meet my modern-day Battista,'' he agreed softly.

He parked the Ferrari in a turnout above the crashing surf and eyed the fog-shrouded beach. ''I think this is going to be an indoor picnic.''

''It's all right. I don't have any objection to dropping crumbs on your nice leather seats.''

''In exchange for which privilege, you could at least tell me what's of interest in those eighteenth-century tourist letters," he murmured, reaching behind the seat for a white sack.

"Ah hah! I knew it! You're trying to find out what's on that film!"

"Well, I can't deny that I'm curious," he soothed, handing her a Styrofoam cup of coffee and arranging the croissants carefully on a napkin. "I'm not asking for details, just a general idea...?"

Alina hesitated, torn between the need to gloat and the need for secrecy. She wrestled with the two for a while and finally compromised. "The English tourist," she stated with barely repressed excitement, "appears to have stayed at the villa which had once belonged to Battista."

There was a thick silence. She knew that in spite of his claims, Jared was suddenly, fiercely alert.

"Before it was gutted by fire?" he breathed as if hardly daring to ask for clarification.

She nodded with a triumphant smile. "And there was a library..."

Jared whistled silently, croissant forgotten. "Oh, my God!"

"And this wonderful, unremembered tourist wrote letters home to a friend, telling him what he was discovering in the library," she concluded kindly. "Things about a certain former owner of the villa..."

Jared manfully swallowed a large swig of coffee, clearly trying to act as nonchalant as possible. He didn't fool Alina for a second. She remembered her own indescribable thrill when she'd first realized what she was on to. He was going through the same thing.

She watched him drag himself back under control and hid a smile.

"Have you—" He broke off and tried again. "Have you had a chance to view the film?" He sounded as if he were walking on eggs. Cautious.

"No. I'm going to take it down to the library and use one of their microfilm readers. It's going to take a lot of time because there's bound to be a considerable amount of unrelated information in the letters, and you know how hard it is to read that eighteenth-century handwriting. I'll start on the project early next week. I don't want to be rushed."

"No..." The remains of the Styrofoam cup disintegrated between his fingers. Jared looked blankly down at the crushed plastic as if not quite realizing he'd done it.

Alina's smile broadened. He glanced up and caught it, and his glance flashed with enigmatic warning.

"If," he began coolly, "I give you my word not to dangle you by the heels out over the surf until you agree to let me see the film, will you promise to have dinner with me tonight?"

Her laughter was uncontainable. It bubbled over

in triumphant, elated glee. "Poor Jared!" she taunted lightly, warmly, understandingly.

He brushed the remains of the cup from his slacks, deftly whisked the croissant from her lap, and yanked her lightly across his knees. "Not so poor," he growled, holding her trapped between his chest and the steering wheel. "You've got the answer to what happened between Francesco and Battista, and I've got you. It all comes to the same thing in the end."

"Not a chance!" she retorted bravely, aware of the electric excitement flowing through her even as she tried to struggle up from the confining embrace.

He drew tantalizing fingers down the line of her throat, his gaze turning very green. "It's been a long time since I made love to a woman in the front seat of a car."

He eased her head back onto his shoulder and took her lips, gently crushing her cry of protest.

Four

Her protest having been made, Alina resigned herself to the kiss with rueful understanding. She knew exactly what was going through Jared Troy's head, and she understood completely. He was really doing very well to limit his outward signs of frustration over her possession of the film to a mere kiss. If the situation had been reversed, Alina knew she would have seriously considered giving herself the satisfaction of pushing him into the ocean.

Unable to move as his mouth swept down on hers, Alina told herself to be patient. There was no point fighting him. What could he do to her in the front seat of a car? No, she was safe enough for the moment, and after a while he would have worked off some of his natural and understandable aggression....

But even as she let herself relax against him, Alina knew she was becoming far too conscious of the hard body against which she nestled. Beneath the fabric of his shirt she sensed the strength in him. And as she lay sprawled across his thighs, the urgent, demanding maleness of him pressed against her.

Alina stirred with belated uneasiness, but as she did so the gently crushing kiss began to change, invoking the brief passion she had first experienced at his hands the previous evening.

Her feelings of triumph and of having the upper hand because she held the film wavered. The impact of the sensually increasing desire in Jared started to blot out the facts of the situation, filling up all the space in her mind with a demand that she acknowledge his need.

His lips moved on hers, deeply, with a lazy aggression that told her he was confident of the eventual outcome. As confident as Francesco had been of Battista. She lifted her hands, intent on levering herself away from him, only to find them caught and carefully held.

"It's a small enough price to pay, isn't it?" he growled huskily against her mouth. "You owe me something for the way you got that film..."

Alina turned her head aside in annoyance. "I don't owe you anything!"

"You're wrong. You've promised so much during the past three months...."

Before she could argue the point further, he was invading the intimate warmth of her mouth, his tongue seeking to mate with hers. When she lost her patience and knew the next thing to go would be her willpower, Alina began to fight back.

Deliberately she used her teeth on his marauding tongue, sinking her amber-frosted nails deeply into the pin-striped shirt at the same time.

He winced at the sudden punishment and she heard the muttered oath as he momentarily drew away.

Wordlessly he examined her challenging, warning expression, his eyes narrowed and thoughtful. "The arrogance of a woman," he finally rasped, "can be incredible. No wonder Francesco was reduced to beating Battista!"

"He never...!"

This time her words were cut off by the flash of ruthless dominance which washed over her. The gentle demand was gone from his kiss as he forced her mouth open once more and used his teeth not quite gently on her lips.

In spite of herself, Alina acknowledged that she might have deserved the small attack. She also knew with sheer feminine intuition that it would cease as soon as she surrendered. Jared wanted her. He didn't want to fight her for the embrace.

As that fact registered, another shock awaited. Jared's hand moved boldly, possessively to her breast, slipping inside the chamois leather jacket to close warmly over the soft curve.

Caught between the realistic knowledge that she was ultimately quite safe here on a public beach and the mounting level of beguilement filling the confines of the car, Alina stopped struggling. She let the waves of his desire wash over her and knew, even as she did so, that she was glorying in the power she seemed to have. Something told her that Jared Troy did not lose his self-control easily.

"You are so exactly as I imagined you would be," he breathed, ignoring her small attempts to restrain his fingers as they found the buttons of the chambray shirt. "So exactly what's been missing in my life."

When he slid his fingers inside the blue shirt at last, gliding unerringly across the slope of her breast to find the exquisitely sensitive nipple, Alina sucked in her breath and found herself arching into him.

"I need you," he whispered throatily as she buried her face against his shoulder. He kissed the curve of her throat and trailed stinging little caresses around to the nape of her neck.

His fingers coaxed forth her nipple, bringing it to

a taut erectness which seemed to spark her whole
body into greater awareness. Convulsively Alina's
hands gripped his shoulders, and she turned her head
blindly to find the curve of his shoulder, pushing
aside the open collar of his shirt.

"Oh!" she cried, the small sound nearly stifled by
the unfamiliar pressure of increasing sexual urgency.

The betraying shiver slid down the length of her
body, and she knew Jared felt it. At once his hand
stroked more deeply. He found the softness of her
stomach with caressing fingers.

Tracing delicate, arousing patterns on her skin, he
worked around the curve of her waist, pulling the
blue shirt free and pushing it and the chamois jacket
aside.

In another moment she lay exposed to his hungry
gaze, her breasts hardened into betraying peaks. With
a groan he shifted her slightly, bending his head to
curl his tongue around the firm nipples. His hand
found the sensitive base of her spine and probed luxuriously beneath the tight jeans.

Alina almost didn't recognize the moan, found it
hard to believe it had issued from her own throat.
Jared wasn't the only one who was losing his self-
control, she thought crazily. An unfamiliar desire
threatened to leave her shivering and helpless in his
arms.

Reality began to slip farther and farther out of

reach. The world compressed itself, telescoping into the front seat of the black Ferrari. A curiosity unlike anything she had ever known began to goad Alina, urge her to further discoveries. The closest emotion she could identify it with was the consuming inquisitiveness she'd had to probe every aspect of the life of Battista and Francesco. But the sensation was more immediate, more electric than the curiosity she had about the two Renaissance lovers.

Coming alive under his touch, Alina moved against Jared's hardness, finding the crisp hair of his chest as she fumbled with the buttons of his shirt. His slightly incoherent response only served to arouse her further. She began to string kisses along the line of his collarbone, kneading his chest like a cat as she moved lower against him. He buried his lips in her hair as she finally touched the tip of her tongue to the flat male nipples, and the groan of response came from deep within his chest.

"Touch me," he pleaded hoarsely. "I've dreamed of it for so long...."

Lost in a whirling universe of sensation that fed off the driving demand of his obvious need, Alina spread damp little kisses across the tanned chest while her hands worked against the firm flesh of his waist and back.

She felt his touch along her thigh as he explored the curve of her, knew he wanted to be rid of the interfering fabric of her jeans. When his hand stroked over her hip and back down she found herself seeking the throbbing hardness beneath his slacks with her own fingers.

His response was sharp and immediate. As if she'd pulled the trigger of a gun, he froze.

The next thing she knew he was pulling her reluctantly but firmly more erect, cradling her against him while he buttoned her shirt with surprisingly unsteady fingers.

"Not here," he whispered with a trace of shaky amusement. "Not on a public beach. I want privacy and all the time in the world. After waiting this long, it's going to be right, not rushed!"

"Jared...?"

She looked up at him through her lashes, instinctively seeking some explanation for her own response. It had never been this sudden, this uninhibited. She knew herself capable of what she thought of as a normal degree of affection, but this had been far beyond normal!

"I know, I know," he soothed achingly, finishing the task of rebuttoning the blue shirt and beginning to stroke her with long, consoling movements from shoulder to thigh. He pushed her head down on his shoulder, and his mouth twisted in a tender little smile.

"What do you know?" she husked.

"I know how you feel," he said simply. "I expect this is how it was for Battista and Francesco. They didn't stand a chance of ignoring each other once they'd met. And neither do we. Don't look so shocked," he added with tender humor. "I'm as caught up in this as you are. It wouldn't take much for me to forget all my good intentions and take what's mine here and now."

"What good intentions?" she managed, reacting to the sure possessiveness in his voice by struggling awkwardly out of his loose grasp and settling into her seat with an annoyed flounce. "I didn't notice an overabundance of good intentions just now!"

He watched her, green eyes still full of an unsatisfied hunger. "I told myself it should be done right. Candlelight and wine, more of the conversation we've already started in our letters, all the trappings. A woman like you should be wooed and won on several levels. Don't you think I know that? I'm not an idiot. I know that it's no good unless I have all of you."

She stared at him, wanting to scoff or tell him to go to hell, and totally unable to do either. Alina felt trapped, mesmerized by the spell he was weaving. "Why should you want all of me?" she finally asked on a thread of sound.

"Can't you guess? Don't you know you're the one person who can fill the empty places in my life?

More than that, you're the one person capable of making me realize what it is to be lonely. I need you. I want you. I won't be satisfied until I have you. All of you. There is nothing else I can say, no simpler way of expressing it. My need is so great that it took me three months to work up the courage to come and get you. The fear of finding out that the woman I had come to know through her letters didn't really exist was paralyzing. But when you opened that door last night, I knew she was real."

She reacted to the utter certainty in him with a woman's instinct for self-preservation—Battista's instinct. "Jared, it doesn't work like that, and if you'd read my letters as carefully as you say you have, you'd know it! Your interest in me hinges on our quarrel over Battista and Francesco. Perhaps in some way you've identified me with her, I don't know. Perhaps you've identified yourself with Francesco. But don't think that, like him, you can bully your way into my life...."

"He didn't force his way into Battista's life. Not the first time. You yourself admitted he seduced her," Jared said meaningfully.

"Well, forewarned is forearmed! I'm not going to let you seduce me!"

"Don't be afraid of me...."

"I'm not afraid of you, dammit!"

He appeared to consider that. "No, I don't think

you are. It's yourself you're worried about, isn't it? You've got your life arranged just the way you want it, and you're afraid of letting me into it. But am I such a risk? You know who I am. You know a great deal about me. I'm not a passing stranger. We've corresponded for three months, and now I'm here to meet you in person. All I'm asking, for the moment, is that you spend the day with me and have dinner with me tonight. Is that too much? After all we've shared for the past three months?''

"You're trying to coax me into a relationship which I have no interest in pursuing...." she began resentfully, knowing she was already responding to his lures.

"Just think, instead of arguing with me on paper, you can have the satisfaction of making all your points in person," he prompted. "Surely you're not going to admit you can't handle me. What would Battista say?''

In spite of herself, Alina felt the sudden laughter in her threaten to spill over. Her hazel eyes were lit with it as she regarded her tormentor.

"You're not fooling me for a minute, you know. I realize you're deliberately trying to back me into a corner from which my pride will allow only one exit. I'm quite familiar with your various techniques of getting me to agree with you. You've used them all in your letters! But they won't work any better in person than they did through the mail!''

He sighed. ''Perhaps. But they're worth a try. Can you really resist the opportunity of spending the day arguing with me about Battista and Francesco, though?''

Alina tipped her head to one side, once again, now that he no longer held her, aware of a feeling of being in command of the situation. And she had the confidence which had come since her disastrous marriage had terminated. Alina was very accustomed to having things go her way. She could manage herself and her life. ''You have a point,'' she drawled.

A slow, mocking grin revealed his own half-buried laughter. But the expression in the gem-green eyes was one of undeflected determination. ''I know,'' he said. Then he flicked a casual glance out the window, satisfied for the moment with his small victory. ''The fog's clearing. How about a drive up the coast? It's been awhile since I saw the ocean.''

''Nobody said you had to live in Palm Springs!''

''It suits me. Most of the time.'' He switched on the powerful engine and put the Ferrari in gear.

Something occurred to her. One of the insignificant little things which shouldn't have mattered to her one way or the other.

''How do you run your business from Palm Springs? Have you an office there?''

"I have a portion of my home set up as an office. I operate alone, you see. I follow the market activity with a small business computer, and I have a couple of telephones. It's all I need."

"A regular cottage industry," she quipped, thinking of the rumors she'd heard of his success in the commodities and stock markets. Quick, decisive kills and then total disappearance from the scene for a while. Ruthless, hard, and very, very shrewd.

They wound their way through the now sunny, elegantly Spanish-style town by the sea. Following a few directions from Alina, Jared guided the car along the streets that ran closest to the water. They passed secluded, exotic beachfront homes, busy motels catering to tourists, and acres of green parks. Stretching back up into the hills, the Spanish architecture of the town's homes gleamed brightly in the morning light.

"How did you wind up in Santa Barbara?" Jared asked at one point as they drove through the green hills above the sea.

"I moved here right after graduating from college. I decided that since I was finally going to have to face the real world to some extent, I would make sure I had a pleasant view of it!"

He chuckled appreciatively. "A picture-postcard town, all right. Did you have a job lined up?"

"No, but I knew I wanted eventually to open a bookstore. I went to work for Nick Elden...."

"I thought you two were partners?"

"A couple of years ago Nick let me buy into his business. He's taught me so much!"

Jared looked as if he were digesting that remark carefully. "Does the book shop deal only in rare books?" he finally asked neutrally.

"No, we're a very diversified store. New and used and rare. Nick has a genuine flare for finding buyers and sellers in the rare-book trade. We've found some absolutely unbelievable things for people. A wonderful copy of Samuel Johnson's *Dictionary of the English Language* from 1755 came across my desk just the other day. And I found a first edition of Bram Stoker's *Dracula* for a client who specializes in collecting horror stories. You should see it," she added with a laugh. "It was bound in bright yellow cloth with blood-red lettering!"

"That was printed about the turn of the century, wasn't it?"

She nodded. "We've had some very early Spenser and Milton and a couple of sixteenth-century books of manners. Lovely stuff," she added with a satisfied sigh.

"You're fortunate to have a career which blends with your own personal interests," Jared observed quietly, his eyes on the road.

"Don't you enjoy making money?" she retorted cheekily.

"It's a means to an end." He shrugged. "I happen to be reasonably good at it, but I can't say it gives me any great pleasure."

"Just allows you to buy the things you want?" she finished for him.

"Some of them," he admitted with a sidelong glance that said a great deal. "Not all."

"Not me," Alina verified carefully, lifting her chin with a touch of aggression.

"No, unfortunately," he agreed. "It would make things much simpler if that were the case!"

Satisfied at having made her position clear, Alina relaxed a little further, taking pleasure in the day and the drive. As if a truce had been declared and accepted, the conversation flowed easily between them. As easily as it did between old friends, Alina thought at one point, masking her amusement.

To her surprise they didn't wind up arguing about Battista and Francesco after all. For some reason the two passionate footnotes to history took second place in Alina's mind to the unexpected interest she found herself taking in her modern-day *condottiere*.

There were questions she found herself asking which she would never have asked through the mail, little things which shouldn't really have intrigued her in the first place. Her own curiosity was strangely unnerving, but not nearly so unnerving as the realization of just how much she did know about him.

There were moments when she could almost read his mind, and it was those instances which made her wonder just how much she had learned about him through his letters. She had, indeed, been reading between the lines!

He took her home eventually, driving past the lovely old Spanish mission church and winding up the hillside beyond to where her condominium was perched.

"I'll be back in a couple of hours," he said, leaving her at the door late that afternoon. "Time enough?"

"To dress for dinner? Yes." She watched him go, taking a subconscious pleasure in the smooth coordination of his movements as he slid into the car. Five hundred years ago he would have mounted a horse or climbed into a carriage with just that degree of ease and assurance. A vital, healthy, gracefully strong man. For the first time she allowed herself to wonder about his love life. Almost at once she backed away from the issue. A man like that would not lack for female companionship.

So why, she wondered again later as she dressed with more than her usual care, had she always assumed him to be an isolated, even lonely man from his letters? He himself had confirmed this.

She chose a full-sleeved burgundy velvet dinner dress that fell below her knee. The wide, romantic sleeves were caught in narrow cuffs stitched in gold. A metallic gold sash wrapped her waist, gently emphasizing her slenderness. The V-neck accented the simple gold chain at her throat, and she concluded the gold touches with a clip that held her softly folded hair. Battista would have liked the outfit. Catching sight of herself in the mirror, Alina winced ruefully as she remembered Jared's comments on her clothes the night before: barely restrained opulence.

But when she opened the door to him later she was fiercely glad she had chosen the burgundy velvet. Nothing less would have done justice to her date for the evening.

Jared's basically conservative taste was evident in the fine, dark material of his suit, but the outfit had the sleek, close-fitting look of Italian design. It emphasized his lean, rangy strength so well she knew it must have been handmade. A subtly striped shirt and coolly marked silk tie also had that European look and fit. The cocoa dark hair was still damp and carefully combed and Alina had to fight a horrifying urge to ruffle it with her amber-tipped nails. The thought brought a flush to her cheeks, which stayed there as she saw his slow smile of appreciation. There was no denying they were thoroughly pleased with each other.

"Both of us may have been reading a little too much Italian Renaissance history," she said lightly to break the thread of sensual tension that hung in the air between them.

"On us it looks good." Jared chuckled, handing her into the black car. "Aren't you going to ask me where we're going? Santa Barbara is, after all, your turf. I'd have thought you'd be worrying about an outsider not knowing where to take you for dinner."

"Frankly I hadn't thought about it," she admitted, savoring the close intimacy which enveloped the small cockpit as he slid in beside her. "You would have asked for suggestions if you'd wanted them."

"You know me so well," he murmured lightly, switching on the ignition.

She started to make a flippant reply, found herself hesitating, and said instead with a kind of wonder, "Sometimes I think I do. It's strange, isn't it? This afternoon I felt as if we'd known each other for—"

"A good three months?" He grinned.

Alina laughed and the mood of the evening was set. He took her to the elegant lounge and dining room of an old-world hotel by the sea. As with almost everything else in Santa Barbara, the architecture was unmistakably Spanish, with cool vistas opening onto charming gardens. The cuisine and service, however, were continental. After a pleasant discussion of the possibilities on the menu, they settled on spinach salad with a sizzling hot dressing, scallops mousseline accompanied by paper-thin slices of smoked salmon and sautæed cucumbers, and a kiwi-fruit tart for dessert. The wine was a pale Riesling from one of the exotic little boutique wineries of Northern California.

The candlelight gleamed on the snowy tablecloth and polished the silver. It threw heavy, mysterious shadows on Alina's burgundy velvet and burnished her gold jewelry. And it seemed to her that Jared's eyes turned more and more into emeralds every time he looked at her.

"Tell me," she asked midway through the scallops mousseline, "how did you come by your interest in Renaissance military history? A holdover from your college years?"

"I'm afraid there wasn't anything to be held over from my college years," he said quietly. "I went to work straight out of high school."

Alina, who hadn't bothered to date a man in years who didn't share her academic background, thought about that. "Doing what?" she finally asked curiously.

"Running errands for Vittorio Molina," he told her calmly, but the emerald eyes gleamed.

The slice of sautéed cucumber on the end of Alina's fork fell ignominiously to her plate as she flinched in reaction. She shut her eyes in rueful despair. "I never stood a chance. No wonder he called you to ask why you wanted a microfilm of those letters.''

"He was a little curious as to why I hadn't asked for them myself," Jared admitted dryly, sipping his Riesling and watching her with barely concealed amusement.

"Oh, dear."

"I told him you were tracking down information for me from any available source and simply had pursued the letters on your own. Which was the truth as far as it went."

"I feel like an idiot! I guess I would never make it as a black-market art dealer. Little mistakes like that could destroy that sort of career!" Jared's mouth quirked but he said nothing, watching as she mulled over her faux pas. "Running errands for him, hmmm? What sort of errands?" she asked finally, anxious to change the conversation.

"Molina is one of the most brilliant financiers I've ever met. He took me on as an assistant and taught me everything I know. His art and rare-book collection is an integral part of his life, so it became a part of mine."

"What happened? I mean, you don't still work for him...."

"We had what could be termed a parting of the ways," Jared explained deliberately, his eyes on the wine in his glass as he swirled it gently.

Alina tried to figure out exactly what that meant. "You wanted to go off on your own eventually?"

He looked up. "Yes."

She frowned. "Was he angry when you left? Did he think you should have stayed with him?"

"We parted amicably. There were no hard feelings because I left before our independent natures came into severe conflict." Jared grinned dryly. "I think he knew our relationship had reached a point where I would have to go off on my own. I was no longer an apprentice. He gave me his blessing and a very beautiful copy of Baldassare Castiglione's *Courtier*."

"To sort of round out your education?" Alina chuckled, thinking of the famous Renaissance book of manners which had influenced Western social behavior to the present day. *The Courtier* covered everything from table manners to bedroom manners.

"It's a very useful book, you'll have to admit," Jared said with a small laugh. "Castiglione was well aware of the need for gamesmanship in a gentleman's behavior! Vittorio Molina understands such things. And he approves of the Renaissance ideal of the worldly, broadly educated man who can do everything with that easy nonchalance the Renaissance termed *sprezzatura*."

"And which we, today, have downgraded to the phrase 'being cool,'" Alina concluded. "So you had

a humanist's education, after all.'' The notion of a
liberal arts or humanistic education had begun in the
Renaissance.

"I'm afraid so. Not as formal as yours, perhaps,
but rather varied when I think back on it. Did you
major in history in college?''

She nodded. "But it didn't really become a passion until I started working in the book shop. Ex-
posure to the rare materials Nick handles bred a kind
of obsession in me. And for some reason that obsession focused on the Renaissance.''

There was a short pause and then Jared asked carefully, as if he had to know, "This Nick Elden. Has
he tried to become more than a teacher and partner?''

Alina's head came up at once, her eyes cooling.
"Nick is a friend. I owe him a great deal.''

"Did you plan to take him as a lover one day?''
he persisted grimly.

"If I did, it wouldn't be any of your business,
would it?'' she retorted, goaded.

"Of course it would. I have no wish to come home
some day and find I'm obliged to call him out,''
Jared murmured baitingly.

She saw the humor in his eyes and told herself he
was merely teasing her. She could give as good as
she got. "You're not taking a truly Renaissance approach to the subject, Jared. Romantic intrigues, in-
fidelity and seductions were very important to courtly

life! A major source of amusement. Probably took the place of television.''

He gave her his rather dangerous smile. ''The intrigues and seductions were considered all very well when it came to another man's woman, but a lover took good care to keep a vigilant eye on his own!''

''No one kept an eye on Battista! She was her own master!''

''Until Francesco came along,'' Jared reminded her firmly.

''I have a feeling it's time to change the topic again,'' Alina stated grandly. ''If you want to discuss someone's love life, talk about your own!''

''I thought you'd never ask.''

She bared her teeth at him and then quickly had to change the expression to a polite smile as the wine steward approached to pour more Riesling into their glasses.

But when the man had turned away from the table with a small bow, Jared's eyes had sobered. He leaned forward intently. ''There is no one else in my life, Alina. I was married once. It happened when I was about thirty, and like yours, the marriage was a mistake. I was a businessman and I made a business arrangement with a beautiful woman who thought she would be happy marrying a successful man and being his hostess. The arrangement failed. Largely, I think, because we were incredibly bored with each

other right from the start! She left me to marry a
much more dashing, jet-set acquaintance, and I was
vastly relieved to see her go. End of story.''

Alina stiffened at the bluntly told tale. ''I'm sure
you haven't been totally alone since your marriage,''
she managed coolly.

''Yes,'' he stated categorically. ''I have.'' He saw
the disbelieving look in her widening eyes and shook
his head impatiently. ''There have been nights in the
beds of other women, but they meant nothing. I
didn't particularly want them to mean anything. I
wasn't even conscious of my loneliness until I found
myself eagerly awaiting your letters. I was thoroughly shaken the day I realized I was actually
watching for the mailman!''

Unthinkingly Alina's mouth curved upward as she
recalled the eagerness with which she received the
letters postmarked Palm Springs. She had told herself
she was merely interested in the next skirmish over
Battista and Francesco, but deep down she knew
there had been more to it than that.

The sensual tension that had hovered around them
all day quickened, compounded by the flickering sensation of mutual recognition. It was, Alina thought
later as she went into his arms on the dance floor, a
little like meeting someone you had known once before very long ago. Five hundred years ago?

Five

It was inevitable, Alina decided later, that she would invite him in for coffee. And it was probably equally inevitable that Jared would accept the invitation as if he had expected nothing less.

She served it to him, a rich aromatic brew laced with a fragrant liqueur, and placed a plate of tiny, exquisitely rich chocolates on the glass-topped coffee table in front of the white banquette where they sat.

"I have to leave in the morning," Jared said abruptly, breaking the soft silence.

She glanced up, meeting his eyes over the gilt rim of the tiny white coffee cup. The rush of disappointment appalled her. How could she possibly feel this

way after such a short time? But she had given up
seeking answers to such questions. They had been
plaguing her all evening, and there were no easy ex-
planations.

"I see."

His eyes softened as he studied her. She sat with
one leg tucked under her, the burgundy velvet spread
gracefully around her. The small, wine-colored shoes
she had worn lay abandoned on the rug beneath the
coffee table.

"It's business," he elaborated. "Something which
can't wait. I'll be back as soon as I can."

"Will you?" she asked gently.

"Nothing on earth could keep me away."

He set his cup and saucer down on the table, the
emerald eyes darkening as he reached to take her cup
out of her hand and place it beside his.

Without a word he pulled her to him, and Alina
went, her doubts and uncertainties falling aside as his
lips took hers.

This time she gave herself up to the swirling magic
that he wove around them. The day had been so
good, the evening so perfect, and she felt she knew
him so intimately on so many levels....

With a sigh Alina surrendered to the need and
longing in him. Jared felt her body soften in his arms
and groaned, making no secret of his desire. "You
have given me so much today and this evening," he

rasped, his mouth sliding with clinging warmth across her own. "And all I can do is ask for more. I find I am a very greedy man."

His hands moved on the velvet of her dress, molding the outlines of her body beneath it. Slowly he leaned back along the cushions, pulling her on top of him. The burgundy dress cascaded in soft folds across his slacks as he settled her legs between his own.

She lay along the length of him, vibrantly aware of the hardness in his thighs, the buckle of his leather belt as it pressed into the material of her dress, and the urgent but carefully restrained want in him. It was as if he feared to push too fast and too hard. As if he wanted everything to be right...

Somehow his determination to make love to her so perfectly weakened her resistance still further. Unthinkingly she wound her arms around his neck, succumbing to the incredible lure of him. It had been working on her all day, she realized dimly. And now she could no longer fight it. This must have been how Francesco had affected Battista, disrupting her coolly ordered, graciously structured life.

Jared accepted her growing surrender with the gratitude of a truly thirsty man, drinking in the wine of her lips with unflagging desire.

His mouth feasted on hers, deepening the kiss with a ravishing seductiveness that put all thought of the future out of Alina's mind. The hypnotic effect was a seduction in itself. She was rapidly discovering the indescribable sensation of genuinely uncontrollable passion. It was a sensation she had never known. The almost casual demands of her husband had never reached her at these levels.

Slowly, wonderingly, she sank deeper and deeper beneath the waves, her mouth flowering beneath Jared's, allowing a moist, hot intimacy as his tongue found hers.

When she began to respond, her lips making demands of their own, her arms tightening around his neck, Alina felt Jared suck in his breath heavily, his body arching upward against hers. He cupped her curving hips and pulled her tightly into his heat.

"Leaving you in the morning will be the hardest thing I've had to do in a long time," he grated fiercely as he sought her earlobe with questing, tantalizing, gently nipping teeth. "Will you come with me?"

"I...I can't," she breathed helplessly. "My job..."

"I know, I know," he whispered resignedly. "I'll be back as soon as I can."

"Let's not talk about it," she pleaded, tasting the tanned skin of his throat with the tip of her tongue and inhaling the warm, musky scent of his body.

"No," he agreed. "We'll talk about the future later...."

She felt the zipper of the velvet dress slowly, lovingly lowered and then the touch of his slightly calloused palms on the bare flesh of her back. It sent tremors of excitement through her.

Her rioting senses urging her on, she began unlacing the silk tie around his neck, sliding it free with a teasing sensuality that elicited another surging movement of his body against hers.

Slowly, driven by a sudden, inexplicable desire to tease and taunt the man beneath her until his passion overrode his restraint, she undid the buttons of his shirt, and when he was free of it, she wrapped the tie once again around his neck. She held a silk end in each hand and used them to draw fragile patterns in the roughness of his chest hair.

"That tickles," he murmured, half in passion and half in warning humor.

She bent to kiss his shoulder, her body flowing over his.

"You said Battista was the ultimate tease," he grated deeply. "But you seem to have studied her techniques!"

"Instinct," she murmured lightly, using her teeth with tiny savagery on the muscle of his upper arm. It was a delight to feel him come alive, to realize he was in danger of losing the self-control he was striving to maintain. A delight she would never have dreamed would appeal to her.

"Even the professional tease met her match," he reminded her roughly, his hands sliding along her back to her derriere as he explored beneath the opened zipper of her dress.

"Are you threatening me?"

"More than you can even guess."

Heedlessly she stirred against his thighs, feeling the hardness of him and glorying in it.

"Ah!" he growled huskily, and with a swift, impatient movement he stripped the dress down to her waist, leaving her utterly naked above the hips.

Alina shivered from the coolness of the room and the raging green fire in the eyes which went to the tips of her breasts.

With easy mastery Jared shifted, moving her beneath him, his body settling on hers with a heavy, sensual weight that nearly took her breath away.

"Oh, yes, please!" Convulsively Alina wrapped her arms around his back beneath the opened shirt, her eyes closing in delirious surrender to the wash of physical sensation which enveloped her.

He kissed her tightly closed eyes and then the line of her cheek. Slowly, passionately, he worked his way down her throat to the slope of her breasts. There his mouth plucked at the eager nipples until they grew hard and taut.

When he was at last satisfied with the reaction of her body he moved lower. Alina felt the burgundy dress being pushed over her hips, out of the way of the advancing touch of his hands and his lips. Her lacy underpants and sheer pantyhose followed the dress.

Her fingers wound themselves in his dark hair as he strung teasing, inciting little kisses along her waist and over the soft mound below.

When he drew his nails lightly along the vulnerable inside of her thigh she moaned, one knee lifting convulsively alongside him and her toes digging tensely into the white cushion.

"Jared, oh, Jared!"

Her husky plea provoked him further, and he turned his lips into the silkiness of her inner thigh. She felt the gentle, stinging nip of his teeth and shuddered.

Slowly, with a rising tempo that nearly drove her out of her mind, he wove a dancing pattern over the most intimate core of her passion. Head thrown back, her body arched with the tension of a bowstring, seeking more and more of him.

She cried out when he suddenly drew away, getting to his feet beside the white couch. But almost at once he was bending down to scoop her naked body high against his chest.

Her mind spinning, she clung to him, her head

nestled on his shoulder as he carried her with sure
instinct down the hall to her bedroom. He stopped
first at the door of the study, however, and chuckled
softly as he realized his mistake.

"Wrong room," he murmured, striding on to the
right one.

The moment of lightness agitated faint warning
bells in Alina's dazed brain, causing her to lift her
head and open her eyes. He looked down at her as
she lay in his arms, obviously seeing the traces of
uncertainty which had come so belatedly. Then he
was settling her gently on her feet beside the bed.
His eyes never left hers as he yanked the white bed-
spread with its brilliant crewel embroidery down to
the foot of the brass bed.

Then his hands cupped her face with rough gen-
tleness. "No," he half pleaded, half ordered. "You
wouldn't do that to me."

"Do what?" she whispered, knowing he knew of
her sudden doubts.

"You would not play out the role of the quintessential tease. Not tonight. Not with the one man on
earth who needs you so badly!"

His words tugged at her, destroying the faint wave
of doubts. He wanted her so desperately, and she
wanted him. Even Battista had felt this way once in
her life. Now, at long last, Alina understood why her
Renaissance mentor had succumbed to Francesco.

"No," she breathed, her hands gliding around his waist to rest on the leather belt. "Not with you. Not tonight…"

She felt rather than heard his groaning sigh of relief and masculine exultation. He folded her close, his embrace momentarily not passionate but almost reverential. It was enough to convince Alina she had made the right decision.

Slowly, letting the wonder of the moment take her completely, she undid the belt, easing down his zipper and letting him step quickly out of his clothes. When at last they stood fully nude together beside the bed, Alina thought she would become delirious with the electric desire which shot through her.

They touched each other with undisguised pleasure, Jared finding the most intimate curves of her softness while Alina explored the thrilling hardness of his tightly drawn body. Lovingly her hands cupped his maleness, bringing a hoarse sound of need from his lips.

Slowly she sank to the floor in front of him, her fingers kneading the muscles of his thighs and calves as she reigned kisses down the length of his body.

"My lovely Alina," he husked, his hands burying themselves in her hair as she knelt in front of him. "You are more than I had dreamed you could be. I think I've been waiting for you for five hundred years."

He lifted her to her feet, kissing her with deep passion as he found the junction of her tapering legs with one questing hand. A hiss of satisfaction escaped him as he found her waiting secret. "You are so warm and welcoming, my lady. I can't wait any longer for you."

"Yes," she managed in a broken whisper. "I need you so much... More than I had ever realized a woman could need a man."

He picked her up again and set her gently in the middle of the brass bed, and then he was lowering himself on top of her, easing his strong legs between hers with passion and power.

Slowly, with an infinitely erotic grace, Jared completed the final embrace, his body joining with hers so completely Alina could not imagine ever being a single, finite individual again. There would always be some fleeting, inseparable reminder of this moment of sharing. It would be with her the rest of her life.

With a savoring intensity, the passion between them escalated, the rhythm of the timeless bonding claiming them both. Alina heard the little moans and cries that issued from the back of her throat, felt them swallowed by his hungry mouth.

Her nails raked lovingly down his back, conveying her growing urgency as an unfamiliar tautness grew in the region below her stomach. Her hands clenched almost violently around the muscular male buttock as the tension in her rose, crying out for a release which could only be provided by the man holding her so tightly.

"Jared, oh, Jared!"

He must have heard the questioning, pleading tone in her words because his hands smoothed roughly over the skin of her rib cage, down to close under her hips, and pulled her even more tightly to him. "It will happen, darling," he assured her thickly. "Just let it happen."

She believed him, in that moment she would have believed anything he said. But she didn't know quite what to expect. Never had she felt such sensual straining in her own body. The affection that had characterized the first months of her marriage was a pale reflection of genuine passion. It had been easy to set aside the memories of her husband's weak embraces. Jared's loving mastery of her body would never be forgotten.

Trusting him, she clung, letting her body react and rejoice. And then, quite suddenly, the ultimate convulsion claimed her with thrilling power, stealing the very breath from her body.

Instinctively she clutched at him more violently than ever, and with this evidence of her satisfaction singing its siren song, Jared could no longer resist giving way to his own completion.

His throaty exclamation of fulfillment mingled with hers as together they plunged over the brink and began the long, languid fall back to the dark, warm reality of the bedroom.

It was a long, pleasant time before Alina felt like stirring. When she did so, carefully stretching her legs which lay trapped under Jared's, the warm arm lying across her breasts tightened.

"Going somewhere?" Jared murmured indulgently.

"I don't have to. This is my bedroom, remember? I'm home."

"So you are. And so am I." She heard the satisfaction in him and wondered at it. Did he really feel that way?

"Jared?"

"Hmmmm?" His voice was the sleepy, satiated sound of a lazy male lion.

"Do you think this is the way it was between Battista and Francesco?"

He chuckled, his lips in her unbound hair. "I know it was."

"How do you know?"

"Are you always going to be this chatty afterward?" he asked interestedly.

"I don't know yet. There haven't been enough afterwards to see if a pattern is going to develop," she retorted tranquilly, wiggling her toes and peering down the length of her body to watch them.

"There will be," he promised complacently. "Now it's time you went to sleep."

"Why?"

"Because it's very late and you have totally exhausted me!"

"Oh."

"Don't sound so pleased with yourself," he ordered, enfolding her still damp body. "I'm the one who did all the work of getting you where you belong."

"In bed with you?"

"Correct."

"Are you hungry or anything? I've got some milk in the refrigerator...."

He placed a gentle palm firmly over her mouth, levered himself up on one elbow, and planted a deliberate kiss on her nose. "Go to sleep," he growled.

Alina eyed him for a moment through her lashes, saw the humorous determination in the green gaze and, with a sigh, closed her eyes.

When she awoke it was still dark. Morning had not yet come, but as her sleepy senses took stock of her surroundings and the memories returned she realized she was alone in the bed.

Alone, and it wasn't yet morning. Where was

Jared? Surely he wouldn't have left like a thief in the night?

Anxiety coursed through her, bringing her to a sitting position amid the sheets as she glanced around the shadowy room. Where was he?

Restlessly she slid out of bed, pulling the green robe from the closet and belting it quickly around her waist. It was only as she nearly stumbled over the pool of his clothes on the floor that she breathed a sigh of relief. He was around somewhere. The kitchen?

But the light that was on was the one in her study, she realized as she entered the hall outside the bedroom. Curiously she walked to where the door stood half open and pushed it inward.

Jared stood there, gloriously, unabashedly naked, a glass of water in one hand as he studied the portrait on the wall. His head turned as she silently opened the door. Instantly the green gaze warmed as he took in the sight of her tousled head and sleepy body. "Miss me?" he murmured.

"I thought you were supposed to be exhausted," she observed.

"I recovered. Got up for a drink of water and wandered in here to take a look at the portrait I thought I'd seen earlier when I carried you off to bed. Battista, I presume?"

Alina smiled self-deprecatingly. "I like to think

so. The picture fits my own mental image of her. What do you think?'' She came to stand beside him as he turned his gaze back to the elegant woman on the wall.

"I think," he drawled, settling an arm around her shoulders, "that you and the woman on the wall have a great deal in common. So, yes, it must be Battista."

Alina chuckled. "Have you got a snapshot of Francesco?"

"Not exactly. But I have a small copy of Donatello's *Gattamelata* which I think might bear a striking resemblance." He grinned.

"The 'Honeyed Cat,'" Alina translated, thinking of the famous equestrian statue of the powerful *condottiere* Erasmo da Narni. It had been the first bronze equestrian statue on such a large scale to be made since ancient times. It stood outside the church of Sant' Antonio in Padua. "Why did they call him that?" she asked suddenly.

"He's supposed to have had a temperament which combined kindness and cunning. He was a professional in every sense of the word, and it shows in Donatello's statue."

"A professional. Is that how you think of Francesco?"

"It's the highest compliment one can pay such a man." He shrugged. "Come on, let's go back to bed.

I can think of better things to do right now than discuss Battista and Francesco.''

She smiled invitingly up at him, aware of the hard nudity of his body. ''I thought you were in need of rest.''

''I told you, I've recovered,'' he drawled. He set the half-finished glass of water down on the small table by the door as they left the room, and arm and arm they walked back to the bedroom.

Standing once again beside the rumpled bed, he unbelted the sash of the green robe and eased it off her shoulders, his eyes drinking in the sight of her as she stood naked before him.

''I think,'' she whispered huskily, twining her arms luxuriously around his waist, ''that 'Honeyed Cat' would be a good description of you.'' She purred softly.

His mouth lifted in sexy humor as he ran his hands down her back to the base of her spine. ''You and Battista,'' he growled, ''certainly know how to handle men. Just be sure that you save all your compliments and talents for me!''

He lifted her onto the bed, gathering her close as he came down beside her. Alina turned into his arms with delicious anticipation....

He left in the morning, as he had said he must. But not before he had shared breakfast with her in the garden.

"I'll be back as soon as I can," he promised a little roughly as he kissed her good-bye. "And then we must talk."

"Yes," she agreed, hazel eyes shining in the morning light. "We must."

Six

"Alina! I just had a call from a free-lance scout who thinks he's turned up a Wise forgery of a Tennyson book of poems!" Nick Elden hung up the phone behind the vast wooden desk which dominated the far end of Elden and Corey Books.

Alina glanced up from a bibliography she was studying, grateful for the interruption. Her mind had been refusing to focus on her work with its usual concentration. Memories of the previous night kept flitting through her head. Memories of warmth and passion and...love?

She saw the pleased delight on Nick's handsome face, his silvering head nodding to himself. "That's great. I've been looking forward to seeing a real Thomas J. Wise forgery! Is this one of his better ones?''

"Not his masterpiece; most people still think his forgery of the reputed Reading edition of *Sonnets by E.B.B.*, supposedly published in 1847 by Elizabeth Barrett Browning, is the finest thing he did. But this Tennyson could be a good one.''

"Incredible to think that Wise's forgeries now often bring more than the originals!'' she marveled. "He was a master of his craft, wasn't he?''

"Definitely.'' Nick smiled, shuffling through some papers on his desk. "He was a fine bookman in his own right. Started out as a clerk in London and developed the fatal taste of book collecting. He concentrated on nineteenth-century authors and became quite an authority on several. His bibliographies of Tennyson and Elizabeth and Robert Browning are still standard works in the field. His scholarship was impeccable, and he did much to popularize systematic bibliography. You have to admire the man. He had a facility for discovering rare editions.''

"And when they were not to be discovered, he manufactured them!'' Alina grinned. "He died in the thirties, didn't he?''

"Thirty-seven, I believe.''

"Where did the scout find the Tennyson forgery?''

"A private collection in Arizona. He wants us to

handle it. On a commission basis, of course. I think
I have a couple of possible buyers in mind...." His
fingers drummed momentarily on the huge desk as
he considered the possibilities. "Yes, I think I'll start
with Miller. He's been after me for another forgery."

Alina watched her partner reach for his phone
again, and then she quietly went back to her work,
wondering what Jared was doing now. Had he
reached Palm Springs yet? Was he thinking of her?

Her mouth twisted wryly. It was ridiculous. She
was acting like a love-struck young girl instead of a
reasonably sophisticated woman of thirty who knew
all about marriage and the falseness of men. What
she hadn't learned from her own experiences, she'd
learned from Battista. Hadn't she?

The carefully annotated bibliography of the works
of an eighteenth-century author blurred in front of
her eyes as she thought of the man who had so reluctantly left her bed this morning. He was different.
She knew it in the deepest part of her being. No man
could hold a woman as he'd held her, look at her the
way Jared looked at her, unless there was far more
to his need for her than the physical satisfaction of
a night in bed.

But the thing which still amazed her most about
last night was her own response. It had been easy to
avoid becoming involved in a string of affairs since

her marriage. She'd taken no risks because there had been no real temptations.

She'd treated men very much the way Battista had treated them. She had enjoyed their company and attention, flattered them intellectually, entertained them, and made it absolutely clear she had no interest in marriage. In essence, she decided honestly, she'd treated them rather like pleasant toys. They thrived on it. And none of them had ever been in a position to betray her since she'd been divorced.

She'd been lucky, Alina supposed, in the one serious betrayal she had experienced. Her ex-husband had given her a relatively cheap lesson on the subject. Her pride had been hurt, along with her confidence in her personal judgment. She'd felt like a fool, but she hadn't been wounded deep in her heart. The emotions she'd had for her husband weren't strong enough or binding enough to allow that, thank God. He hadn't, she realized much later, been the great love of her life.

But if Jared were to do such a thing to her... No! She wouldn't think of that. Jared was an intent, sincere and utterly honest man. She knew it! Her flowering emotions toward him were safe. It was strange after all this time to be seriously thinking of one man and one man only.

And what was he thinking of her? She bit her lip, remembering one of his statements that first night when he'd shown up at her party. *"Who,"* he'd asked her, *"said anything about marriage?"*

But he'd told her he'd come to claim his lady. His remark on marriage must have been a natural male defense against her ranting at him.

For that matter, she asked herself grimly, what was she doing thinking about marriage? She'd never wanted to remarry. Life was too pleasant, too well organized, and she was much too involved with her work and her socializing to want to change.

She was supposed to be modern and sophisticated. What was the matter with her that she found herself thinking in terms of marriage after one night in bed with a man!

But last night hadn't been just a casual fling and she knew it. Alina would never have been tempted by a casual fling. She had gone to bed with Jared Troy because he had woven a kind of magic around her. A magic she would never have dreamed existed. And once he'd made her his, the soft magic had become steel bonds. She felt deeply and utterly committed.

It was frightening in a way. Thank heaven Jared was the kind of man he was. For Battista the magic had come with a man who couldn't be trusted. Alina shuddered.

The shop soon filled with browsers, and business became pleasantly brisk. Customers wandered down the long, ceiling-high shelves of old books, sometimes becoming lost for hours. Others pored over the really choice items housed in glass cases, and still others hovered around the collection of newly published materials.

By the end of the day, Alina was feeling restless. She knew she was in serious danger of heading straight for home and then sitting around the house all evening waiting for a phone call from Jared. The thought made her grimace. Alina Corey did not allow herself to wind up in such situations!

He was probably expecting her to do just that, too, she decided. He'd kissed her good-bye with such open possessiveness that morning.... Determinedly Alina took a grip of herself. Whatever she felt for Jared, she would not allow herself to behave in such an insipid fashion. She was a woman who had a full life to lead in her own right, and she would not start behaving totally irrationally simply because she might be on the verge of falling in love!

On the verge? Or already well entrenched in the quicksand of that dangerous emotion? She didn't want to think about it closely, she realized as she drove home after work.

The phone was ringing as she walked in the door, though, and in spite of all her good intentions, she found herself flinging down her purse and racing for it.

"Hello?" She wished her voice didn't sound so breathless.

"Alina? This is Brad...."

"Oh, Brad." Desperately she tried to keep a naturally lively touch in her words. What a stupid reaction this sudden depression was! "How are you? Did your poet friend enjoy the party?"

"Of course he did. Everyone always enjoys your parties, you know that. I'm calling to see if you'd like to have a drink down at the marina this evening. It's been a hard day at the university," he added with a theatrical groan.

"Budget cuts?" she asked, smiling.

"No, one of my students is about to publish a paper which I wish I'd written. It's unnerving!"

She laughed. "I can imagine."

"So come and comfort me. Doesn't a nice Margarita while we watch the sunset over the ocean sound enticing?"

"Delightful, but I don't think I can make it tonight..." Alina's voice trailed off regretfully. To her own astonishment she realized she was turning down the invitation because she simply didn't want to be with another man, even though he was only a friend. She didn't want to be with anyone tonight, except Jared. Barring his presence, she felt like being alone. And Alina usually did exactly as she liked. "Can I take a rain check?"

"Oh, sure. But it's tonight my ego needs boosting." he coaxed hopefully.

"You'll survive. Think of it as a tribute to your teaching abilities. The little twerp couldn't have done it without your brilliant coaching, now could he?"

"That's a thought." Brad chuckled ruefully. "I suppose I ought to take that attitude."

She said a few more soothing words about his intellectual prowess and somehow Brad hung up the phone on a more cheerful note. Alina replaced the receiver with a quirking smile and glanced at the clock. She'd have a bite to eat and then...

She remembered the tiny canister of film in her desk. How on earth could she ever have forgotten? That's what she would do tonight. It would get her out of the house and give her something to occupy her mind totally. The library would be open until nine, and she could use one of their microfilm readers.

In a far lighter, more focused mood now that she had a goal for the evening, Alina changed into a pair of jeans and a ruffled plaid shirt. She made herself a salad piled high with fresh mushrooms and then, carrying the salad with her, went into the study.

She opened the desk drawer and picked up the little black canister, tossing it jubilantly into the air and catching it with her free hand. A slow, wicked smile shaped her mouth. It was going to be fun proving her point to Jared. Exciting in a way.

But she realized she no longer had the urge to clobber him in print. In fact, Alina thought wonderingly, perhaps the article could be written as a collaboration. They could publish the ending of Battista's and Francesco's story together.

She thought of the pleasant hours of work ahead and pictured the two of them nestled cozily in front of a microfilm reader, comparing notes. Sitting down behind the rolltop desk, she set her plate aside and twisted off the gray top of the little black can. Idly she peered into the dark interior. And froze.

At first she couldn't believe the film was gone. Alina blinked and quickly turned the can upside down, shaking it fruitlessly. It was gone! The microfilm copy of the letters from an eighteenth-century English tourist in Italy was gone!

Stunned, she stared at the offending canister, a thousand thoughts ricocheting around her head. A thousand thoughts and the one which came inexorably to the surface was the memory of Jared standing naked in her study, staring at the portrait of Battista on the wall.

Alina sat very still, vaguely aware that her fingers were shaking as she placed them on the desk in front of her and lifted her eyes to the picture. How long had he been in her study last night before she'd awakened? Long enough to search her desk?

But he hadn't had the film with him when she'd discovered him, she reminded herself almost hysterically. No, logic said, but once he'd located it there would have been no trouble returning to the study that morning and removing the film. He must have had it in his pocket even as he sat drinking her cream-laced coffee and eating her scrambled eggs!

The shock of his treachery was worse than she could have imagined. Helplessly she met Battista's knowing gaze.

"No," Alina whispered to the portrait, "he wouldn't have done that. He wouldn't have seduced me just to get the microfilm. He's not that kind of man!"

He's another Francesco, the woman on the wall seemed to say. *You said it yourself, remember?*

But that was before she'd gone to bed with him. Before she'd learned of his tenderness and his passion....

A slow rage began to build inside Alina. A rage unlike anything she had ever known. In that moment she knew how Battista had felt when Francesco had calmly walked out of her life after taking everything she had to give.

At first there were tears. Tears of anguish over the

betrayal, and then tears of self-disgust at her own stupidity, and finally tears of rage.

But the tears soon died and left the fury to burn in a dry heat. How could she have been so stupid? Alina asked herself again and again. She hurled the empty canister at the door of the study, watching it bounce onto the carpet and wishing it had been aimed at Jared's head.

She'd probably never get the chance to throw anything at his head. She'd probably never see him in person again! He wouldn't be coming back to Santa Barbara, that was for certain. He wouldn't dare!

The next time she would hear from Jared Troy would be when he dropped her a line to tell her his article on Francesco's affair with Battista had been accepted for publication!

The only consolation she would have would be that the ending of their story wasn't going to please Jared. But all the same, she didn't want him to have the satisfaction of being the one who concluded it in print.

Damn it! She didn't want him to get away with what he'd done! And if she worked fast enough, he might not be able to do so.

Deliberately forcing herself to calm down somewhat, Alina leaped restlessly to her feet, thinking. He couldn't know, she thought, that he didn't hold the only copy of those letters. On Friday when the microfilm had arrived she had taken the elementary precaution of having the master duplicated and stored in her safe-deposit box at the bank.

At the time she'd had no thought of protecting it from theft. She'd only been concerned with keeping the master copy in perfect condition. There was always the possibility that the film would tear while it was being wound through a microfilm reader, or any number of other small disasters could occur. The film Jared had stolen was only a copy.

It wasn't much, but it would be sufficient to prevent him from having exclusive access to what was on that film. She wouldn't be able to take her time now. She would have to work hard in order to beat him into print, but she just might be able to make it.

But try as she would to whip her flagging spirits into a competitive mood, all Alina could remember was the betrayal. How could Jared have done this to her? How could he have used her like this? It hurt her, enraged her, made her want to strangle him. Never had her emotions been so heated and so violent. Never, except for last night...

The closest parallel she had to her present feelings was the depth of emotion she had experienced in Jared's arms the previous night.

That thought only served to increase her fury. The memory of her surrender was almost more than she could stand. The anger was not an antidote to the passion she had known, it was merely the other side of the coin.

My God! she thought, coming to a standstill in her living room and staring blindly at the fireplace. I was falling in love with the man! I've been falling in love with him for three months and last night...

She squeezed her eyes shut in utter dismay. Last night had been the unexpected, joyous culmination of a curious three-month courtship. At least, that was how it had seemed at the time.

But she'd been wrong—very, very wrong. Just as Battista had been wrong.

The phone rang and Alina whirled to stare at it. It couldn't be Jared. Surely he wouldn't call to gloat? Or would he?

She watched the instrument as if it were a snake, letting it ring twice more. Brad perhaps? Hoping to convince her to go out with him after all? Reluctantly, her hand trembling ever so slightly, she lifted the receiver.

"Yes?" The single word was stark, hollow sounding.

"Alina?"

"Jared!" Her breath caught in her throat. "Jared!" she said again, her voice rising.

"What's wrong, honey? Are you all right?" He sounded worried, she thought crazily, genuinely worried.

"Funny you should ask," she managed bitterly.

His deep voice turned abruptly hard, impatient. "Alina, what the hell's the matter? You sound as if..."

"How do you expect me to sound, you bastard?" she heard herself shriek. No! No! She wanted to be cold and diamond hard. She didn't want to lose her temper like this! She didn't want him to know how much he had won.

"Stop it, Alina," he ordered, as if he were dealing with a hysterical female. Which was precisely the case, she thought. "Calm down and tell me what's wrong. Dammit, I wish I were there," he added in a rough growl. "Now settle down and tell me what's wrong. You were perfectly fine this morning when I left. Surely you aren't coming apart at the seams without me already?" The last bit was added in an obvious attempt to lighten the mood.

"Of course I was fine this morning. That was before I realized what you'd done to me. I was right, wasn't I? You're a reincarnation of Francesco! Hard, ruthless, using a woman and then walking out on her. How dare you do this to me, Jared Troy! I trusted you! I *trusted* you," she said again on a wall.

There was a pause on the other end of the line as if Jared were honestly trying to figure out what had happened. Was he going to keep up the act? Didn't he realize she'd found out what he'd done?

"Alina," he finally said steadily. "I'm coming back to Santa Barbara. I told you I'd be back. Surely you don't think I walked out this morning with no intention of returning?"

"Oh, you walked out all right. Taking my film with you! I never would have believed it of you, Jared! Even during the three months in which we wrote those letters I would never have guessed you'd resort to…to seducing me and then *stealing* that microfilm! I thought you might be angry with me for the way I got it. I thought you might even try to bully me into giving it to you. I *even* thought at one point that you might try to seduce me into giving it to you. But I never thought you would be capable of actually stealing it!"

"Stealing the film! I don't have a clue as to what you're talking about! Now calm down and tell me what's going on. Are you trying to tell me the film is gone?"

"You know damn well it's gone! You stole it!"

"The hell I did! Alina, you're going to have me losing my temper in a minute if you don't start behaving rationally. Tell me what's happened. Take it from the top, one logical step at a time. And if you don't get a grip on yourself and give me the whole story in one coherent sequence, I swear I'm going to…"

"Going to what? You've got a nerve threatening

me after what you've done!'' There was no point even trying to control her temper now, she realized vaguely. She had lost all of her self-control. ''But I've got news for you, Jared Troy. You haven't won completely. You're not holding the only copy of that film!''

''I'm not?'' he asked dryly.

''No, you damn well are not! I had a copy made of the master the day I got it. Took it down to a local lab and had it run off. The master is sitting in my safe-deposit box, you…you thief! And I'm going to work night and day on it! You're not going to be the first one to get the end of the story into print! And to think I was on the point of offering to collaborate with you!''

''You were?'' he inquired very carefully.

''Does that give you any great pleasure? Does it give your male ego some sort of thrill knowing you had me completely fooled for a while? Did you make love to me just for the sake of putting a little icing on the cake of your victory? Or did you need the time in my bed in order to have a chance to search my study for that film?''

''I see.'' Jared sounded suddenly thoughtful. ''I'm supposed to have found the film in your study? Last night, presumably, while I was looking at Battista's portrait?''

''There's no need to keep up a pretense of innocence! I went to get the film out of the can tonight and it was gone. I know all about it, Jared! I swear to God, if you were here right now, I'd throw something at you!''

"The slop bucket?" he suggested wryly.

"For starters! I could strangle you, do you realize that?"

"Hell hath no fury…" he began to quote gently.

"I'm not a woman scorned. I'm a victim of theft! You're nothing but a…a crook! A cunning thief who softens up his victims with seduction! The 'Honeyed Cat' was a better name for you than I knew, wasn't it? I'd phone the police and have you arrested if it weren't…" She broke off, gritting her teeth in dismay.

"If it weren't for the fact that you obtained the film under false pretenses in the first place?" he murmured coolly.

"Don't try to wriggle out of this by placing the blame on me! What I did to get that film wasn't nearly as bad as what you did to take it from me!" she cried righteously.

"Were you really going to offer to collaborate with me?" he asked after a moment.

"Go ahead, throw my stupidity in my face! I suppose I deserve it. But that's all the satisfaction you're going to get, Jared," she vowed seethingly. "I'm going to write the last article on Battista and Francesco, and it's going to prove that she never let him back into the villa! I know it is! I know it more certainly now than I ever did before!''

"Because you're feeling as betrayed as she felt?''

"You don't have to sound so kind and understanding, dammit! You're not fooling me, you know. You haven't got a kind, understanding bone in your whole body. You're a lousy thief! A bastard of a *condottiere* who uses a woman and takes what he wants. I should have known! I *did* know! I don't know why I let you do this to me...." To her horror, Alina heard a suspicious break in her voice. She would not cry! Not anymore.

"Is that everything?''

"What do you mean by that?'' she snapped.

"Is that the whole story? The entire list of accusations? I'm supposed to have walked off with your microfilm this morning?''

"After...after seducing me!'' she reminded him vengefully.

"That was the best part,'' he retorted dryly.

Alina gave an inarticulate exclamation of rage. "I'm warning you, Jared Troy, don't ever come within striking range of me again. Don't ever try using Elden and Corey Books for your searches, either. Don't write any letters and don't think you're going to be the first one into print!''

"I hear everything you're saying, and you know

damn well I'm going to ignore all of it. I'll be in
Santa Barbara tomorrow night, and we'll sort this out
once and for all.'' He sounded so arrogantly sure of
himself Alina could have screamed.

"You can go where you please," she bit out, "although I'd be happy to make a few suggestions along
that line, but don't think it's going to do you any
good to show up on my doorstep again! I don't even
know why you should want to come back to Santa
Barbara! You've got what you came for!"

"Not quite, apparently," he remarked quietly.

"Don't tell me you think you can play Francesco's
role right out to the end!" she retorted scathingly. "I
told you once I learn from my mistakes." A sudden,
horrible thought struck her. "And if you think you're
going to seduce me all over again so that you can
get your hands on the master of that microfilm,
you're out of your mind!"

"The only thing I want my hands on at the moment is you! If you think you know how Battista felt,
you can bet I'm fully aware of what must have been
going through Francesco's mind. I told you once he
probably used his belt on her once he got back inside
the villa!"

"He never got back inside!" she yelped, incensed.

"Yes, he did. Just as I'm going to get inside tomorrow night," Jared snapped with a rough edge to
his voice which told her very clearly he was rapidly

slipping over the edge of impatience into outright masculine wrath.

"Never!"

"And when I do," he went on, ignoring her defiance, "I'm going to make you eat every single one of your words. I did not steal your precious microfilm, you little shrew! Although I will admit to one accusation," he added grimly. "I did spend the night in your bed. And I'll be spending tomorrow night there, too! Wringing one apology out of you after another!"

He slammed down the receiver before Alina could have the satisfaction of doing it first.

Hurling the instrument down, she glared at it, wishing she could have thrown it at Jared's head. How dare he? How did he dare to do this to her?

With a groan of disgust, she flung herself into the cushions of the couch. He dared because he was arrogant, ruthless, hard, and every bit the *condottiere* she had first thought him to be! She had made the same mistake Battista had made.

Had Francesco seemed to be the other half of herself to Battista? Had he made passionate love to her, made her feel as if she were the most important thing in the world to him? Had he told her that only she could fill the strange loneliness within him? Had he used his mind and his body to seduce her completely?

It must have been like that, Alina thought sadly. How could either she or Battista have resisted?

But there would be no second chance, Alina swore to herself. She and Battista might have been swept off their feet once by men who didn't fit the normal male mold, who knew exactly how to get past all the carefully erected barriers. But it would not happen a second time!

Jared would not be permitted back into her life twice. She would not allow him to savage her beautifully structured life-style again!

Seven

Alina awoke the next morning with a sweeping sense of relief as she remembered the invitation to an exhibition at a local gallery. It was for that evening, and if ever she needed an excuse to be out of the house, this was the time. Celeste Asher, the artist, was a friend, and Alina had meant to attend anyway. But there was no denying that the exhibition was a marvelous reason for avoiding the possible confrontation with Jared.

Not that he was really likely to show up, she reminded herself again and again throughout the day, so it wasn't as if she were actually running away.

She was still telling herself that as she dressed for

the evening. It was just that if he did choose to appear on her doorstep for whatever ego-oriented reason, she simply had no wish to deal with him and his protestations of innocence.

Going to Celeste's painting exhibition wasn't the only excuse available to her that evening. She could have spent the time making good on her vow to begin studying the microfilm master stored in the safe-deposit box. But even though her mind had returned to the problem often during this afternoon, Alina hadn't been able to bring herself to go down to the bank and fetch the film. Now, of course, it was too late. The bank had closed hours earlier.

Somehow, in spite of all her firm intentions to begin work on the film as quickly as possible, she wasn't yet able to face the prospect. The knowledge that Jared was undoubtedly winging his way through his copy only depressed her further.

But her anger was still riding high, she realized grimly, as she took stock of herself in the mirror. It was the safest emotion she could allow herself at the moment, and she deliberately kept the embers fanned.

It did serve to add color to her cheeks, she thought unhappily. Her hazel eyes seemed unnaturally bright, flecks of gold glittering with a metallic hardness. The edge of her mouth twisted sardonically. The expres-

sion in her eyes went well with the overall image she
was projecting tonight.

The black, high-necked blouse paired with an
elongated, narrow black skirt echoed the hard, re-
mote look. She wore only the wide silver and turquoise belt as jewelry and sleeked her hair into a soft
knot behind one ear. She looked exactly as she
wanted to feel: icy and controlled.

Convinced she had made the right decision, Alina
walked into the crowded gallery a short time later.
She was at once engulfed in the muted, self-
consciously chic atmosphere. A large number of people, dressed to rival Celeste's brilliantly colored,
light-filled canvases, milled about, drinking champagne and making terribly insightful comments about
the paintings. The champagne was obviously being
dispensed with a free hand, and as Celeste had often
observed privately to Alina, such largesse did much
to promote the intellectual, insightful comments.

"Alina! You made it. I was so hoping you would
come, darling. Here, have some of the bubbly and
then I want you to meet Jeffrey...."

"Hello, Celeste." Alina smiled, accepting the
champagne from the tall, statuesque painter. Celeste's wealth of startling red hair had been brushed
into a voluminous chaos, framing her attractive features and making her look a little like a wild lioness.
Vivid blue eyes snapped with the inner energy which

flowed onto her canvases. Tonight, dressed in a glittering, sequined green gown that emphasized her full bosom, Celeste was as overpowering and as good for the spirits as usual.

"It looks like another success," Alina observed.

"Oh, yes. Randall says I'm going to make a fortune this evening. Isn't it exciting?" Celeste laughed with unaffected delight, steering Alina toward a bearded young man standing uncomfortably in a corner. He was probably four or five years younger than Celeste, who was thirty-three.

"Randall's the owner of the gallery?" Alina hazarded, trying to place the name.

Celeste nodded. "That's him over there, the suave, ever-so-gallant gentleman in the charcoal suit. He's a dear. Rather reminds me of your partner."

"Nick?" Alina smiled in surprise.

"You know, darling, I always expected something more than a partnership to develop between the two of you. Nick Elden seems so exactly your type. Refined, educated, sophisticated. And you have so much in common what with running the shop together!"

Alina blinked, a little at a loss to explain her friendly, yet restrained relationship with Nick Elden. She sipped her champagne reflectively. "Nick and I are friends but there's never been a hint of anything more. He's a very private man in many ways. We've worked together for quite a while now, and to this day I still don't really feel as though I know him."

"Totally involved in his rare books?"

"That's part of it, I suppose. He has a passion for them, but it's not the whole story...." Alina hesitated, frowning slightly as she tried to explain. "I know this sounds ridiculous, but sometimes I have the feeling he's two men. And I know absolutely nothing about the second personality. I can't even claim to have seen it," she added with a laugh. "Sometimes I imagine that when he's not at the shop or socializing, he goes home and becomes someone else entirely."

"He's probably gay," Celeste said knowledgeably.

Alina moved a hand in negligent dismissal. "I'll probably never know. The only thing that counts is that he let me go into business with him and he's been a fantastic teacher. I've done very well as co-owner of the shop. He's been extremely generous about the commissions I make handling rare-book transactions."

"He didn't exactly give you half the shop," Celeste reminded her tartly. "As I recall you had to take out a very stiff loan in order to buy in!"

"It was worth it. Tell me about Jeffrey before you introduce us. He looks distinctly unhappy."

"I found him on the beach two days ago," Celeste

explained airily, her volatile personality immediately sidetracked as she threw an affectionate glance at the young man in the corner.

"A stray piece of flotsam washed up by the tide?" Alina grinned wryly, accustomed to Celeste's fancies.

"He's been a fantastic inspiration to me!" Celeste chided mockingly.

The evening drifted past, and Alina tried to let herself become absorbed in it. She listened attentively while an earnest young filmmaker friend explained to her the intricacies of getting a film accepted at the Cannes Film Festival, remembering to tell him how much he deserved the opportunity. Then she was swept up in a small group of artists who were furiously debating the merits of the New York School of painting. She lost track of the various intellectual muddles she found herself in after that, but didn't worry about it.

Inevitably, however, she found herself winding up the hillside above Santa Barbara, heading home. Celeste's show had been an excellent escape but it hadn't obliterated the main issue. What had Jared done that evening? Had he actually had the nerve to arrive at her door?

The answer lay in the slightly menacing shape of the black Ferrari parked at the curb in front of her condominium.

Alina's first reaction was resigned panic. She had known. Somehow, deep down inside, she had realized he meant what he said.

For a brief moment, the panic washed away the fierce pain of betrayal. It almost made her decide to drive right on past her own home. She could stay in a motel...

But even as she ran through the options, she was automatically braking the car to a gentle stop behind the Ferrari. This was her home and she certainly wasn't going to be intimidated into slinking away in the night!

She waited tensely as she turned off the lights of the car and removed the keys from the ignition. Her hand was trembling, she thought a little dazedly. Of all the silly...

Where was he? Why wasn't he slamming out of the Ferrari to confront her?

Carefully Alina climbed out of the front seat, realizing belatedly that there was no one in the black car parked ahead.

He'd come back, she thought wonderingly as she started up the walk to her front door. He had really come back. Just as he said he would.

Why? She fitted the key to the lock.

The door swung open, revealing a darkened hall and no sign of any lights beyond. Where the devil was he? Playing games in the dark? It didn't seem like Jared. He would be far more direct.

Alina shook her head even as that thought flitted through her mind. She knew him so well, she realized vaguely. Or had the feeling she did. Here she was predicting his behavior on the basis of three months of letters and a night in bed! What an idiot she was!

Unable to figure out what was going on, Alina slipped through the house like a wraith in search of a burglar, turning on lights as she went. With every step she grew more tense, more nervous. What was the man doing to her?

It took several minutes to remember that she had not left the patio light on earlier. But it was on now, she realized quite suddenly, noting the unusual amount of light filtering into the living room from the garden area. Alina walked toward the French doors with a feeling of foreboding.

Jared was waiting in the garden.

He sat at the ornate wrought-iron patio table, casually thumbing through a magazine. Alina stared at his cocoa dark hair gleaming in the light.

The sheer nerve of the man routed her panic. How dare he wait for her like this? He must have circled the row of condominiums and vaulted the back fence into her private garden.

Look at him, she thought vengefully, sitting there as if he had every right in the world.

He looked up suddenly and his eyes locked with hers through the glass separating them. Alina caught her breath at the expression glittering in the green depths, visible even from this distance.

And then he smiled. It was an enigmatic smile, full of grim, masculine determination. Alina felt chilled.

"Well, at least you had the sense to come home alone," he remarked, closing the magazine negligently, his voice carrying easily through the screen of the partially opened window on one side of the doors. "I was afraid I might be obliged to stage the heavy, macho scene with some poor innocent man you might have dragged home as a defense against me."

"I don't need any defense against you, Jared Troy," Alina gritted, angling her chin defiantly. "All I have to do is keep that door locked. If you want to spend the night in my garden, you're welcome to so do. It gets a little cold out there when the fog rolls in, though!"

Jared got lazily to his feet, thrusting his hands into the front pockets of the snug jeans he wore. The jeans were something of a shock. Together with the unbuttoned leather jacket riding over an open-necked plaid shirt, they seemed to add to the subtle menace about him tonight. It was as if some of the civilizing veneer had been removed. A mental image of how Francesco must have looked to Battista when he removed the gaudy court clothes and put on battle dress came unbidden to Alina's mind.

"But I won't be out here by the time the fog comes in, will I?" Jared drawled. "I'll be lying in your bed, listening to you tell me how glad you are that I came back to Santa Barbara tonight."

"Not a chance!"

"Let me in, Alina."

"Give me one good reason," she hissed, hating the prickles of anger and fear which were flashing along her spine.

"I didn't steal your microfilm. What more of a reason do you need?"

"You're the only one who could have! The only one with a motive and an opportunity!"

His mouth quirked upward at that. "You have a point about motive. We're probably the only two people on earth who are really consumed with a need to know what happened to Battista and Francesco. But I'm still saying I didn't take the film. The only thing I had on my mind that night was you."

"What were you doing in my study?" She wished desperately he wouldn't stand there and lie to her. Every fiber of her being was in danger of being seduced into believing him in spite of the evidence.

Her inner weakness made her angrier, more high-strung.

"I told you. I got up for a glass of water and wandered in to look at the portrait." Jared moved, gliding soundlessly closer to the nearest glass-paned door. "Believe me, Alina. You know you want to, anyway. Let me in and I'll remove all your doubts."

She wanted to scream at him not to look at her like that, not to speak to her in that mesmerizing voice. How could she be so stupid as to stand there listening to the man?

"Go away, Jared. You're not going to get another chance to use me!"

He reached out and twisted the handle of the door. It rattled fruitlessly beneath his touch. "Open the door, Alina," he ordered very softly.

Her eyes locked with his a moment longer as she felt the power of his will reaching out to force itself on her. Then, slowly, emphatically, she shook her head in denial. Turning on her heel, Alina walked out of the living room, switching off the light behind her.

She didn't dare stay there challenging him face to face, she realized. She wasn't sure she had the courage to go on defying him. How she could be so humiliatingly weak, she didn't know, but the shakiness of her resolve was frightening. He was right. She wanted to believe him.

Alina had reached the kitchen when she heard the tinkle of carefully shattered glass. She knew instantly what it was. Jared had broken one of the small panes in the French doors.

Whirling, she braced herself against the white tile counter behind her, feeling like a small, cornered animal. She was trembling, and in that moment she couldn't have said whether outrage or fear or some combination of both was the cause. Jared was going to force the test of wills on her. She should have known he would. *She should have known.*

A moment later he appeared in the kitchen doorway, leaning against the jamb with such casual menace that Alina's knuckles whitened. "I wonder," he murmured sardonically, "if it was this easy for Francesco."

Alina swallowed and finally found her tongue. "I doubt it. Battista lived in a violent age. She would have had the villa better protected against unwanted intruders!"

"Am I so unwanted?" His voice deepened huskily. "You wanted me very much the other night."

"Stay away from me, Jared."

He ignored her, leaving the support of the doorway to start forward. "Don't you realize that nothing could keep me away from you? Not after waiting so long and especially not after what happened in your bedroom the other evening."

Instinctively Alina began edging away from him, sliding along the counter, her eyes never leaving his. He changed direction to follow her cautious retreat. He didn't rush her, he simply came toward her with a certain air of inevitability.

"You won't convince me of anything, definitely not your innocence in the matter of the theft, if you...if you attack me," Alina warned breathlessly as the panic began to take hold again.

"I wouldn't dream of attacking you," he said softly. "I'm going to make love to you."

He was closing the distance between them, each step bringing him closer. In another moment or two he would reach out and grab her. In that instant, Alina knew she could not force him to back down. He was bent on subduing her physically, acting on the age-old masculine principle that any woman could be handled effectively by sheer force.

Alina's nerve broke. Consumed by a flaming rage, she swerved, grasping a saucer which rested on the counter top. She flung it at him without giving herself a chance to think. And then she was running, even as the china dish clattered to the floor behind her.

She heard his muttered oath and wondered if she'd managed to hit him with the saucer. He was coming after her now with the long, easy strides of a large cat closing in for the kill. Alina fled down the hall toward the study, the narrow black skirt hampering her movements.

Ducking into the study, she whirled to slam the door and lock it. But she was too late. One large hand caught the door, pressing steadily inward as she braced against it with her full weight from the other side.

"Damn you! Get away from me, Jared! You have no right…!"

"We'll talk about rights later," he informed her, pushing almost easily against the door.

She couldn't hold out against his weight. Frantically her eyes scanned the small room, searching for weapons. Then she leaped away from the door, flinging herself across the short stretch of space to the ceiling-high shelves that lined the opposite wall.

Instantly the door cracked open behind her, revealing a dangerously annoyed Jared. Alina didn't hesitate. She had gone too far. There was nothing to do except to continue fighting. Methodically she picked up the nearest object on the shelf beside her, a little brass candlestick, and hurled it at him.

"Stop it, Alina! So help me, I'm going to use my belt on you after all!" He warded off the flying candlestick with one arm. The green eyes blazed at her as she reached for the cloisonne bowl which had stood beside the candlestick.

"Get out of here, Jared!"

"I'm going to exact full payment for everything you throw at me, you little hell cat!"

The cloisonne bowl whizzed past his head, missing it by scant inches to land with a thud against the wall behind him. Before it had even hit the floor, a small dictionary was sailing through the air.

The male annoyance coalesced into something far more intimidating. Alina saw the flash of cold fury in the narrowed emerald gaze and it gave her a perverse satisfaction to know she had finally made Jared as angry as she was.

"I thought you were different!" she grated accusingly as she picked up the next object on the shelf and aimed it at his chest. "You really had me fooled, you bastard. Did that give you a lot of pleasure?"

The latest volley struck harmlessly against the black leather jacket. Jared ignored it, taking a step forward. The lines of his harshly carved face were set in an attitude of unswerving determination. "What made you think I was different?" he rasped, catching the book which came flying at him. "What made you think I was a man you could trust?"

"I thought you were sincere! An honest man!"

"You thought I was a reincarnation of Francesco! How the hell could you believe I was any better than he was?" Jared challenged, fending off a flying pencil holder.

"For the same reason Battista thought she'd found

a man she could trust, I suppose," Alina yelled in outrage, her breath coming in short pants which flushed her face. "You seduced me! All those letters making me think you were just interested in proving your point about your friend, Francesco, when all the time you were actually seducing me!"

"I was?"

"You know you were, dammit! You led me to think I knew you! Understood you! What's worse, you made me believe you might be the only man on earth who understood me! And then you used that against me. You found my weakness and used it to seduce me! All for the sake of getting hold of that piece of microfilm! I'll never forgive you for that, Jared Troy!"

He struck aside the copy of the Renaissance history journal almost absently, his eyes on the color in her cheeks and the sparks of gold in her eyes. "You've got it backward, you know. You were the one who was seducing me."

"That's ridiculous!"

"I wish it were," he whispered harshly. "But it's the truth. You made me think you might be the one woman on earth who would truly understand me, but that's not the case, is it?"

"I understand you now, all right!"

"No, you don't. If you did, you'd know what your accusations are doing to me!"

"What?" She stared at him, caught off balance by his grimly rasped words. "Don't try to tell me I'm *hurting* you by letting you know I found out the truth!" She laced the words with all the scorn at her command.

"A man likes to think his woman trusts him," he whispered as she faltered over the next object on the shelf.

"I'm not your woman! I'm not any man's woman!"

"You weren't until the night you gave yourself to me," he agreed far too gently. "Alina, you little shrew, put down that bookend and look at me! Do you really believe I'd treat any my woman so badly? Do you really believe I'd steal that microfilm just to one-up you in print? If I'd wanted that film from you I would have demanded it. I'd have made you give it to me. But I would never have resorted to stealing it!"

Alina clutched the bookend, her gaze pinned by his. She could feel her resolve wavering at the pleading in his voice and the still angry sincerity in his eyes. "You must have taken it," she managed breathlessly.

He shook his head. "You know better than that. You know I would have used other means of getting it, don't you?"

He put out a hand and carefully removed the bookend from her nerveless fingers. She barely felt it as her mind churned with conflicting knowledge. There were the facts of the theft to be balanced against the clamor of her instincts. She wanted to believe him innocent. She wanted it so badly she knew she was allowing it to affect her judgement in that crucial moment.

But she couldn't fully deny the knowledge of him she'd gained from three months of arguing with him via letter. It might be an emotional, irrational response, but deep down she knew he was right. He would never resort to stealing. It simply wasn't his style. He had Francesco's own pride, she thought belatedly. Neither man would lower himself to such a petty action.

"Oh, Jared," she whispered shakily, her hazel gaze suddenly betraying the underlying vulnerability. "Are you sure you didn't take it?"

He almost smiled at that, his face softening as he studied her. "Quite sure."

She closed her eyes, drawing in a deep, steadying breath. It was such a risk, such a risk....

"You can trust me, sweetheart," he murmured, not touching her. "I might beat you from time to time, but I would never cheat you. In any way."

The trace of humor in his mild threat reached her senses, and Alina gave a long sigh of relief. Her eyes flicked open, the furious gold sparks melting rapidly. *"Oh, Jared!"*

She threw herself into his arms, shaking with reaction as she buried her face against the leather jacket. He held her fiercely, as if he'd had a very narrow escape, indeed. Without a word Jared molded her to his body, conveying the depths of his own relief as she trembled slightly in hers.

"It's all right," he soothed, stroking the nape of her neck. "It's all right. I know how you must have felt."

"Do you?" she whispered brokenly.

"Don't you think I know you well enough by now to understand what it must have been like for you to find that film gone and me the only logical candidate for thief? You had protected yourself for so long, only to wind up giving yourself to a man who seemed to have stolen everything."

"It wasn't just that you appeared to have taken the film," she agreed in a small, muffled voice.

"I realize that." His hand moved upward, gently pulling the pins from the knot behind her ear. In long, luxurious movements, he let the bronzed brown softness fall free to swing around her shoulders. "Don't you think I know how much you gave me the other night?"

"I was so afraid...."

"But not any longer?" he interrupted, the raw hope plain in his words.

"No, not any longer."

It was the truth. Whatever else he might be, Jared wasn't a thief. She knew that now. How could she have thought he was? In some ways she really knew him very well.

"What are you smiling at?" he demanded in amusement as he sensed her change of mood.

"Our thinking we know each other so well. You were so sure you could talk sense into me, and now I can only wonder how I ever thought you capable of theft. I should have known better. I *did* know better. It was just that I was so angry...."

"With yourself?" he hazarded perceptively.

"I suppose so," she groaned, pulling away to meet his eyes.

"Battista taught you well, didn't she?"

Alina lifted one shoulder in mute acknowledgement of the statement. "Men are safest when they're under control and not allowed to get too close."

"Intellectual pets?" he mocked, eyes gleaming with laughter and something more. Something deep and sensuous.

"Exactly," she confirmed, responding to the look in his eyes. Her lips curved with an unconscious invitation.

But instead of taking her up on it, the amusement

vanished from Jared's expression. "Were you this angry when you found out your ex-husband was sleeping with his female students?"

"You mean did I hurl half the contents of my bookshelf at him? No. I simply packed my bags and left."

"He didn't come after you?"

She cocked her head to one side, hearing the urgency behind the question. "Of course not. Richard was a philosopher. So he accepted my decision. He wouldn't have dreamed of doing anything so forceful, even if he'd wanted me back." And she hadn't wanted him to come after her. She'd felt nothing but disgust over her husband's actions.

"But you knew I'd be back tonight, didn't you?" Jared's hand laced and tangled its way through her hair in an erotic little motion that stirred Alina's nerve endings.

"Yes," she whispered honestly. "I knew."

He nodded in satisfaction. "That's why you were out when I arrived. Where the hell were you, anyway?"

"I take it this isn't the time to tease you and tell you I was out with another man?"

"Not unless you want me to make good on all those macho threats I was making a while ago!"

"I attended a showing of a friend's paintings at a gallery downtown. A *female* friend."

"Ah." He began a slow, seductive smile that caught at her senses. "Thought I'd get tired of waiting for you and go away, hmmm?"

She chewed reflectively on her lower lip. "I told myself that was a distinct possibility. But as soon as I saw the Ferrari in front of my home..."

"You realized what you knew deep inside all along, didn't you? That there was no escape. You were going to have to face me and your own feelings." He bent down and scooped her easily into his arms, holding her tightly against his chest.

"Jared?" A flicker of pain wavered in Alina's hazel eyes as she looked up at him. "Jared, I'm sorry I thought you'd taken that film."

"You just made up for it," he assured her with a dagger grin.

"How?" She frowned, already aware of the tremors of excitement shooting through her limbs as he started out of the study with her in his arms.

"By believing me against all the evidence. You still only have my word on the subject," he reminded her coolly.

She lifted her fingertips to touch the grooves etched into the side of his mouth. "It's enough."

He bent to kiss her throat with warm gratitude. "Thank you, Alina."

Eight

The kiss, which had begun in gratitude, merged with rising passion. Head back, her hair falling wantonly over his arm, Alina closed her eyes in relief and pleasure. The two sensations mingled for a time, leaving her a little dizzy.

She realized she was being carried into the bedroom, but when Jared set her down it was not in the middle of the brass bed. Instead he seated her gently on the white lounge beside the window. When she opened her eyes she found him on one knee in front of her, tugging off her shoes.

She smiled softly, reaching out to run her fingers through his dark hair as he bent over his task. He looked a little rough around the edges tonight, she thought affectionately, surveying the leather jacket and jeans again.

"What's so funny?" he demanded, glancing up in time to catch the flash of amusement in her eyes.

"I was thinking that you came dressed for trouble tonight...."

"And I found it." He let the shoe drop silently to the carpet, the dagger smile reflected in his eyes. "Only now can I truly appreciate what poor Francesco went through! Getting inside the house is the easy part!"

"Don't go drawing any conclusions about Battista and Francesco based on what happened between us tonight!" she scolded, her heart leaping at the expression in his eyes. "It's not the same sort of situation at all!"

"Yes, it is." He put up slightly roughened palms to capture her face and pull her head briefly down to his. "It most definitely is."

He kissed her lingeringly, urging her lips apart and seeking out the warmth of her mouth with hunger and passion. When he released her to go back to his task of undressing her, Alina was trembling.

But she wasn't the only one whose body was reacting so strongly. Jared's fingers were shaking as he began unfastening the buttons of the black blouse. He leaned forward as he slid the material off her shoulders and caressed the unconfined breasts with the softest of little biting kisses.

"It was worth wading through that barrage you hurled at me in the study," he teased gently, cupping her small breasts. "I kept telling myself it would be."

"You were so sure of yourself?" she mocked, knowing her womanly softness was budding into firmly tipped fullness beneath his touch. Her fingers clenched urgently into the muscles of his shoulder, slipping beneath the collar of the jacket.

"I didn't have any choice. I need you too much," he admitted. He stroked the nipples and then his hands slid down to her waist, finding the zipper of the skirt.

In another moment or two she was naked, her slender body gleaming in the pale light of the bedside lamp. Still he knelt on one knee before her, massaging her feet and calves with slow, sensuous motions. As his fingers worked their magic he began dropping damp, heated kisses along her thighs.

The languor of desire stole through Alina's body, narrowing her eyes in heavy-lidded passion and sending wave after wave of erotic excitement down her spine. She loved this man, she realized in an overwhelming flash of certainty. She loved him, and in acknowledging that, she recognized the other truth: she had never really loved before in her life.

That was why it had been so easy to play Battista's game, to convince herself that she had no desire to remarry. She had never really known what it meant to need another person so badly.

Slowly, lovingly, she began undressing him, sliding the black leather jacket onto the floor and fumbling with the buttons of his shirt. He let her take her time until she reached for the buckle of his belt. Then, as if he had grown too impatient to await her ministrations, Jared got to his feet and finished removing the rest of his clothes.

She thought then he would surely move them to the bed, but instead he dropped back down in front of her, the emerald eyes very green and full of uncharted depths as he deliberately, inevitably parted her legs.

Kneeling in front of her he began caressing the insides of her thighs with circling, random patterns that made Alina unconsciously sink her amber nails into the bare skin of his back.

"Oh"

The exclamation was a muffled moan from far back in her throat as his lips began following his fingers. He worked his way upward toward the heart of her femininity, each kiss more lingering and more heated than the last.

"Jared, please…! Oh, Jared, I think I'm going to go crazy…!

"That's how I want you," he breathed, his tongue darting out to taste the warm silk of her. "As crazy as you make me."

With steadily mounting tension, he continued to caress her, sometimes letting his fingers curl deeply into the roundness of her upper thigh, sometimes drawing his nails to delicate detail behind her knee. He was almost worshipping her body, Alina realized with a strange feeling of tenderness. The thought made her catch her breath. He needed her, he wanted her. Was he in love with her? Did he know what love meant? She had only just discovered it herself....

She leaned forward, finding the nape of his neck with her lips just as he closed his hand possessively over the core of her fire. He must have felt the quiver that shook her body at the intimate touch, heard the almost soundless moan of passion that escaped her throat.

He responded to it abruptly. Groaning with deep male need, Jared suddenly shifted, going over onto his back and pulling her down on top of him with unexpected fierceness.

"Come here, my sweet, hot-blooded vixen," he rasped as she sprawled across his hard body. "Show me how much you want me!"

Gone was the worshipful attitude of a moment earlier, and in its place was a ravening masculine hunger. Alina responded to it instinctively, pouring her pent-up desire over him in a wave of tangled bronzed hair and butterfly fingers.

She strung fiery kisses down his throat as he clenched her buttocks, and then she began working her way down his body, glorying in the feeling of power.

Beneath her she felt the thrusting hardness of him and her hands trailed sensuously over his ribs, across his taut stomach and below, seeking to capture and hold him in the most intimate of embraces.

Deliberately she slid across him, tangling her legs with his, until her tongue dipped suggestively into his navel.

"Do you know what you're doing to me?" he grated, snarling his fingers in her hair and holding her to him with a tender roughness that conveyed his need. "I've never wanted a woman as badly as I want you. All these months of thinking about you, learning about you, reading your letters as if they were love notes…"

"Oh, Jared," she breathed. "I've never known what it felt like, never understood this kind of passion, this…need." She had almost said the word "love." But even in the heat of the moment, a tiny voice whispered that it was too soon, the sensations she was experiencing were too fragile. If he didn't use the word yet, himself, she would wait.

"Come close and let me lose myself in you," Jared whispered. His strong hands circled her waist, half lifting, half guiding her until she lay stretched out along the full length of him. Slowly, with inescapable power and tenderness, he fitted her body to his.

When she gasped aloud at the moment of ultimate possession, he uttered something choked and inarticulate. And then he was clutching the roundness of her hips, pulling her into the raging rhythm.

Alina gave herself up to the churning excitement, sensing that Jared was doing the same. Together they clung, giving and taking until their flaring emotions fused into a single, leaping flame that consumed them completely.

It was a long time later before Alina drifted back to reality to find herself still lying on top of Jared, their damp bodies seemingly sealed together. She lifted her head dreamily, reluctantly pulling away from the comfortable resting place of his chest and watched as he opened his eyes with lazy satisfaction.

"You've a nice way of apologizing." He grinned, ruffling her hair. "A man could be driven to great lengths to secure an apology from you."

"That was not an apology!"

"A welcome home?" he tried.

"Something like that." Alina shifted luxuriously, ignoring his warm chuckle. He took advantage of her

slight movement, settling her gently on her back on
the carpet.

One strong hand flattened proprietarily on her
stomach, and the emerald eyes gleamed as they
swept her body. In spite of what they had just shared,
Alina felt herself blushing.

Jared smiled wickedly as he watched the pink
shading rise upward from the swell of her breasts.
Propping himself on one elbow, he bent over to kiss
one rosy nipple. "You'll get used to it," he assured
her.

"Get used to what?"

"Me drinking in the sight of you."

"Will I, Jared?" Alina's eyes glowed with the
depth of her feelings.

"Definitely." There was all the masculine assurance in the world in his voice. He sounded enormously certain of himself and of her.

"You're supposed to look at me with adoring gratitude at this particular moment," Alina told him re-
proachfully.

"Not possessive lust?" He cocked an eyebrow in
mock confusion.

"Absolutely not!"

"I'll try," he promised earnestly, the devil still
lurking in his gaze.

"Something tells me your experience with behavior modification is limited." She sighed.

"Behavior modification is a term for one of your academic behavioral scientists to use. We businessmen are more direct," he explained, rolling onto his back and letting one hand continue to rest casually on her naked thigh.

"You mean that you *condottieri* are more direct," Alina corrected with spirit.

"Ummm." He didn't bother to counter the charge.

There was a thoughtful silence while Jared seemed to gaze absently at the ceiling. Watching his hard profile, Alina knew his mind had gone on to something else. "What's wrong?" she whispered, the humor fading from her voice.

He hesitated. Then he turned his head and gave her a level glance. "You do realize that regardless of what we've just settled between the two of us, we're still left with a problem?"

"I was under the impression men held the view that sex solved everything," Alina attempted flippantly, unsure of his searching expression.

His quick dagger smile came and went but his eyes stayed serious. "Not quite everything. Not in this case."

Alina's mind suddenly remembered the obvious. "You're referring to the little problem of the missing microfilm?" she asked dryly.

"If I didn't take it, Alina, we're left with the question of who did. You were right about one thing. You and I are probably the only two people on earth who care enough about Battista and Francesco to resort to underhanded methods of research.''

She grimaced. ''Are you going to hold my nefarious conduct in securing that film from Molina over my head indefinitely?''

''Only on the odd occasion when I feel it necessary to bring you to heel…. Ouch!''

The exclamation came out on a sharply exhaled breath as Alina punched him lightly in the ribs. ''You were saying?'' she prompted warningly.

''Er, yes. I was saying we're still left with the problem of who would want to take the film.'' He eyed her poised fist warily.

''It could be rather exciting,'' she noted consideringly. ''Until one remembers that no one would have had an incentive or an opportunity to steal it.''

''Except me.''

''Don't start that again!''

''You're really satisfied I'm in the clear, Alina?''

She smiled a very brilliant smile, wondering if the love behind it was terribly obvious. ''I'm satisfied.''

For a moment he simply looked at her, and then Jared seemed to pull himself back to the problem at hand. But not before Alina had seen the flash of something in his eyes which might have been gratitude or relief. Her smile widened invitingly.

''Don't look at me like that, honey,'' he ordered

with a groan. "I've got to think. You said you made a copy of the film?"

"Within a couple of hours of receiving it. I wouldn't have dared to go back to Molina and ask to have the letters refilmed if I'd accidentally wrecked the original on a reader!"

"Oh, you'd have dared all right. Probably would have fed him some line about how your 'client,' namely me, had clumsily lost it!"

"I've learned my lesson in sneaky dealing," she assured him piously.

"I'll bet. Okay, so the film sitting in the safe-deposit box at the bank should be a duplicate of the one that's missing."

"So?"

"So I don't know what we might find when we take a look at it," he went on deliberately, "but I think we ought to do just that as soon as the bank opens in the morning."

"Are you so eager to find out you're wrong about Battista and Francesco?" she taunted.

"No, I'm just eager to find out what it's like collaborating with a researcher who knows how to apologize when the errors of her ways are pointed out to her," he retorted smoothly, pulling her back into his arms with a hunger that was more than physical.

The next day Alina left for an extended lunch with only a quiet word to Nick about needing to conduct

some business at the bank. He'd known she'd commissioned the film from Molina, naturally. She'd
been far too excited at the time of the discovery to
keep it to herself. But he didn't know she'd used
Jared's name to convince Molina to allow the letters
to be microfilmed. She'd thought it diplomatic not to
let her business partner know she'd stooped to such
levels. She also hadn't mentioned the film's disappearance to Nick. Initially because she'd been too
upset with Jared's supposed "betrayal" and ultimately because Jared himself had asked her not to
mention the matter.

"Why not?" Alina had demanded curiously over
breakfast. A tiny frown creased her forehead as she
realized Jared was taking charge of the small inves-
tigation.

He'd smiled blandly, munching a sliced English
muffin. "Will 'because I said so' suffice?"

"Hardly!" she returned sweetly.

He groaned. "Some collaboration this is going to
be with you refusing to get into the team spirit!"

"I don't mind being a team player as long as you
don't insist on being the captain all the time!"

But in the end she'd agreed to follow his advice,
so she didn't mention the fact that the film was missing to Nick.

Her small squabble with Jared over who was in
charge paled into insignificance, however, beside the

shock which awaited her as she eagerly, but gently, wound the strip of microfilm into the library's viewing machine. Terribly conscious of working with the only remaining copy of the film, Alina took great pains to handle it with caution. So much caution, in fact, that it was several seconds before she turned her attention to the viewing screen.

For an instant she simply stared at the first page of what was clearly a book produced during the earliest decades after the invention of printing. A book which dated from the Renaissance itself, not several letters from the eighteenth century.

"Jared! That's not what I ordered. I don't even recognize that! Those aren't my letters!" Alina was unaware of her aggrieved tone of voice as she stared with dismay at the screen. "It's a book printed in Italian, not my English tourist's letters!"

"Probably from the fifteen-hundreds," Jared observed slowly, leaning close to study the archaic printing.

"But why would Molina send me this? It doesn't make any sense!"

The lines at the edges of Jared's mouth tightened intently. "You hired an outside filming company to make the copies on location?"

"Yes, you know how Molina is about letting any part of his collection out of his private library, even temporarily. I hired a mobile microfilm outfit that's done work for our book shop in the past. Nick's used them for years. They take their cameras and equipment to the required location and work on site. They're based on the East Coast where Molina lives, so it didn't cost me all that much. But somehow they must have gotten hold of the wrong material to film. I don't understand it.''

The thought of explaining the mistake to Vittorio Molina and presuming on his generosity so far as to ask for a refilming was upsetting. One didn't presume on people as wealthy and as powerful as Vittorio Molina.

''Already plotting how you're going to ask for another shot at those letters?'' Jared grinned wryly, slanting Alina a sidelong glance. ''Don't forget, you've still got my clout. We'll work out something....'' He broke off, his look of concentration suddenly deepening.

''What's the matter? Do you recognize the book?''

''Yes, I'm afraid I do,'' he replied so softly she had to bend down to hear him. ''It's one of Molina's prize possessions. Very odd, isn't it, that your film crew got this particular item by mistake?''

''Why?''

''It's a very rare, very valuable treatise on Renaissance military history, written by an historian of the time. Molina saved me a lot of money by outbidding me for it when it came up at a private auction last year.''

"How private an auction?'' Alina asked curiously.

"Several of the people who would have given their right arms for this book weren't even invited,'' he told her dryly. "The owner was very particular.''

"I see. Well, that's all very interesting but it doesn't answer our questions. And we're stuck with the wrong film,'' Alina grumbled in disgust. The ending of Battista's and Francesco's story had been so close!

Thoughtfully Jared reached out and switched off the viewing light and began rewinding the film. "We're stuck with the wrong film,'' he agreed slowly, "but we seem to be in possession of a microfilm copy of an item that differs from those letters in one essential respect.''

"What are you trying to say, Jared?'' Alina was having trouble comprehending anything other than her own personal disappointment.

"We agreed that no one else on earth had a passionate interest in Francesco and Battista except ourselves, right?''

"Right.''

"We're now holding a film of a book that a number of people would pay a great deal of money to get their hands on,'' he concluded, dropping the roll of film back into its canister.

"But it's only a microfilm copy of the book, not the original book itself," she protested.

"The pages filmed from the book were not shot at random," Jared explained softly, tossing the little container into the air and catching it neatly as he met Alina's narrowed gaze. "They were the pages which could be used by experts to assure identification of the work as the original and not a reproduction. The pages with small printer's errors and the pages with the illustrations. A prospective buyer would want to examine those carefully before purchase to make sure the item was genuine."

"Perhaps Molina is considering selling the book and had the microfilming crew shoot those pages at the same time they were on hand to film my letters," Alina suggested, brightening at the thought. "If it's just a mix-up, that means his prospective buyer got my letters by mistake. The film company mailed the wrong items to the wrong clients!"

Jared gave her a pitying glance which effectively quelled her rising enthusiasm. "If Molina was interested in selling the book, he would have given me first crack at it. Believe me."

Alina stared at him as he took her arm and guided her forcefully out to the car. "You're trying to tell me the film crew shot that book without Molina's permission?"

"It looks that way. I'm going to call Vittorio as

soon as we get back to your home,'' Jared declared a little grimly as he stuffed her gently into the car.

"But, Jared, I can't go back home. I have to get back to work!''

"I'll drop you off at the shop, then,'' he agreed obligingly, sliding in beside her and starting the engine with quick efficiency.

Alina eyed his profile as he guided the Ferrari out of the parking lot and onto the street. She knew without being told that he was completely wrapped up in this latest twist and wondered at his fierce concentration. "Jared, how badly did you want that book when it came up for auction last year?''

"Very badly,'' he said tersely, not glancing at her.

"*How* badly?'' she pressed with growing conviction.

He shrugged. "Badly enough to ignore the fact that the book's previous ownership is a little cloudy,'' he admitted very softly.

She gasped. "Jared, are you trying to tell me you went into an auction for a book which you knew had been stolen? No wonder it was a very private affair!'' Abruptly she was grinning. "And you had the nerve to criticize my underhanded methods of research!''

"I didn't say it had been stolen,'' he protested indignantly. "And certainly the owner who was offering it had obtained it honestly.''

"Then why the cloudy history?" she demanded pointedly.

"Well, there is some…uh…question as to how the first American owner obtained it…."

"Let's hear it. I want to know all the gory details," Alina ordered cheerfully.

Jared groaned. "I should never have brought up the subject."

"Too late. We're accomplices…."

"Collaborators," he corrected firmly. "Oh, well, if you must know, it's one of the items which apparently was hidden by its European owner during World War II in an attempt to keep it out of Nazi hands."

Alina nodded, remembering that many works of art and historical treasures had been concealed for that purpose.

"After the war it was sold to an American officer. And not, I gather, by the original owner who had hidden it. The officer brought it back with him and kept it quiet, not wanting to have to give it up should the true owner appear and claim it. Since then, it's been sold a couple of times, always very discreetly. No one wants to call attention to the book…."

"In case someone with a claim on it should come forth and demand its return," Alina concluded.

"Right."

"And you'd be one of the first to know if Molina was trying to market it?" she prodded.

He nodded, saying nothing.

"So the film crew must have gotten hold of this by mistake," Alina said slowly.

"Not likely. Nor is it very likely they would film the particular identifying pages they did, either. I'll know more after I've talked to Molina."

He halted the car by the curb in front of the book shop, leaning across the seat to kiss her in what Alina privately thought of as a rather husbandly way. "See you after work, honey."

She climbed out of the car, waved good-bye, and turned to walk back into the shop where Nick looked up expectantly.

"Business, hmmm?" He chuckled in good humor.

Alina winced. "We're collaborating on the Battista-Francesco thing," she explained weakly, hurrying to her desk and hoping Nick wouldn't notice her betraying blush.

"Not a bad idea," her partner observed. "Jared Troy's Renaissance scholarship is first class, and his collection is outstanding. Between the two of you, you're liable to get a lot farther than working alone."

Alina bit her lip, thinking of the surprise which had awaited her this morning when she'd wound the microfilm on the machine. But it was too late to go into a long explanation now. And Jared had asked her to keep quiet about the whole matter. She contented herself with a quick smile of acknowledgment and bent her head over the English bookseller's catalog which she was searching for a client.

The shock which awaited her when she drove home that evening, however, was far greater than the one she had experienced when she had discovered the wrong material on the microfilm.

Instead of greeting her with a drink and a casual explanation of the Molina film mix-up, Jared was waiting with the Ferrari packed. He was carrying her suitcase down the walk as she drove up to the curb.

"What on earth...?" Alina began in stunned amazement as she opened the door of her car. "Jared, what do you think you're doing? Where are you going with my suitcase?"

"You're coming with me to Palm Springs for a few days, honey," he said calmly, putting the case in the car. "I think I've packed everything you'll need. If you're missing anything we can buy it there...."

"Jared! What are you talking about? I'm not going to Palm Springs with you! I have to work!" Alina stomped forward irately, reaching for her suitcase.

Jared stepped into her path, his hands going forcefully to her shoulders. "Honey, listen to me. Something's going on with that book. Something which could be dangerous. Molina is handling matters on his end, and I want you out of the way until everything is settled.''

She looked up into his grimly set features, not understanding. "But what does that have to do with me?"

He drew in his breath, looking as if he couldn't decide how much to tell her. Then Jared seemed to make up his mind. "There's a chance your partner is mixed up in this, honey. Molina is checking things out from his side. But until everything has cooled down, I want you where I can keep an eye on you. And I want you several miles away from Elden and Corey Books.''

"But what's this got to do with Nick?" she wailed, her brows drawing together fiercely. "Jared, please! You're not making any sense!"

"I'll explain everything on the way to Palm Springs," he assured her, giving her a gentle shove toward the condominium. "Let's lock up and be on our way.''

"Stop ordering me about! I'm not going anywhere until I figure out what's happening around here?" Alina declared, her stubbornness rising to the fore.

"Alina, my sweet," Jared returned in a nononsense voice which told her he meant every word. "If you don't get into that car of your own accord, I'm going to put you in it. Understand?"

The *condottiere* was taking charge, Alina thought belatedly. So much for a collaboration.

Nine

"This virtually amounts to kidnapping," Alina snapped angrily as the Ferrari sped down the coastal highway toward Los Angeles and beyond.

"An old Renaissance pastime," Jared drawled, his attention on his driving.

"Will you be reasonable? What in the world am I supposed to tell Nick? How can I phone him and casually say I won't be in for several days?" she rapped.

"Tell him it's a case a true love. You got swept off your feet," he suggested dryly.

Alina threw him a scathing sidelong glance which, by rights, should have inflicted serious injury and probably would have, she decided, if Jared's hide wasn't so tough. Why did he have to make a joke about true love?

"Jared, I'm warning you. I want an explanation and I want it now."

"Okay, okay," he soothed. "It boils down to the fact that Molina has reason to think the microfilming agency you use is occasionally involved in performing a little extra 'service' on the side. A service reserved for very special clients. He's having them thoroughly checked out, but by late this afternoon there was already cause to question some of their activities."

"What sort of service?"

"Assisting in the theft and sale of certain prize books from private libraries," Jared told her succinctly.

"I don't believe it." Alina stared stonily out the window at the ocean on her right. "Nick's used that agency for years."

There was a deadly pause and then Jared said softly, "Exactly."

At the unspoken implications, Alina's head came sharply around. "Are you accusing Nick of illegally dealing in rare books?" she blazed, incensed.

"It's a possibility we have to consider," he began reasonably.

"I don't have to consider it! I've known Nicholas

Elden for years! I wouldn't be where I am today
without him! We've worked so closely, I'd know if
he were involved in anything illegal!''

"Would you?" Jared asked simply.

"Is Molina's book missing?" she charged.

"No. Not yet."

"Well, then? Where's the crime?" Alina demanded triumphantly. "What makes him think
someone's after it?"

"The fact that it was filmed by 'mistake' in the
first place," Jared told her patiently. "There was no
mix-up the day of the filming. Vittorio remembers
your request very well. He also remembers pulling
those letters himself and giving them to the film
crew. They set up their cameras in his library and
shot the letters there. But there was a point at which
he was temporarily called out of the library to handle
some business on the phone. He left his secretary at
the door just as a precaution. But she was only in
charge of making certain no one left with anything
he didn't own. She didn't supervise the actual filming.''

"And Molina thinks the crew took advantage of
the time they had alone in the library to film those
pages out of that history?"

"He thinks that's the only explanation."

"But why?" Alina almost wailed in exasperation.

"To show a potential buyer what they had to sell.

If the transaction was agreed upon, presumably the book itself would have been stolen at a later date. Another advantage the film crew had by filming on the premises was the opportunity of assessing any alarm or protection systems in place around the house and library.''

"But if they shot my letters, how did I wind up with that book instead?''

"Presumably that's where the real mix-up occurred,'' Jared explained quietly.

"Damn!'' Alina's mouth set furiously as she realized what might have happened. "My letters went out to some idiot who won't know what to do with them, and I'm stuck with a few pages from an obscure history! Whoever got my letters will probably toss them in a trash can somewhere!''

"Will you kindly stop viewing this situation from your own personal perspective? We may be in the middle of a major rare-book theft!'' Jared admonished, but not without a flicker of humor as he tossed a quick glance at her unhappy expression.

Rather guiltily, Alina acknowledged the validity of his words. There were more pressing problems at the moment than the lost letters. It was just that having them so close only to be snatched out of her grasp... Belatedly she remembered Nick.

"What gave you and Molina the notion that Nick

is involved?'' she asked haughtily, still angry at Jared's accusation.

"It's just a possibility. Molina will handle everything...."

"What does that mean?'' She glared across the seat at his firmly set chin.

Jared drew a long breath as if debating how much to tell her. "He's going to have his house watched.''

"He's notified the police?'' she asked quickly.

"No, I've told you, no one wants to publicize the book's existence. Molina's hired a very private, very discreet agency.''

"And they're going to watch the house to see if anyone comes back to steal the book, is that it?'' Alina's disgusted tone successfully conveyed her opinion of such an operation. Molina was setting a trap! "It seems to me that I'm the major suspect, not Nick. I'm the one who actually commissioned the film crew to shoot those letters on site!''

Jared said nothing and realization dawned in Alina's racing brain. "Oh, no! Don't tell me you two actually considered me as a suspect, too!''

"Molina mentioned the possibility but I set him straight immediately,'' Jared said quickly.

"Thanks!'' she muttered tartly, chilled at the thought of being even briefly thought guilty of such a thing.

Jared smiled slightly. "I explained to him that you

were far too passionately involved with Battista and Francesco to have thought of anything but those letters. I told him I knew you rather well. Which is only the truth. Elden, on the other hand, is another problem.''

"Why?"

"He's one of a handful of people Molina knows who are aware of the book's present owner. And the order for microfilming in Molina's library came from your firm, don't forget. It's all too much of a coincidence. Elden knew you were having those letters filmed, didn't he?''

Alina hesitated, feeling trapped into a betrayal of her partner. "Yes," she finally mumbled. It couldn't be! Nick couldn't be guilty of such a crime!

"I know you've worked with him for years, Alina," Jared continued gently, "but how well do you really know the man?''

It struck her that this was the second time in as many days that someone had asked her just how well she knew Nicholas Elden. She thought of her answer to Celeste. Nick was an unknown quantity in some ways. That feeling of not knowing what sort of person he was when he wasn't at the shop or playing the gracious guest came back in a wave to flood her mind with unanswerable questions.

"What you're accusing him of doing carries the implication that he used me as a cover for getting that book filmed—virtually tried to put the blame on me in case his actions were ever discovered,'' she finally said carefully.

"Yes."

"I don't believe it. Besides, all of us have been a bit sneaky in this business. I used your name to convince Molina to let me have the letters filmed, Molina and you both bid for a book which might have been illegally obtained years ago...."

"Come on, honey," Jared interrupted impatiently. "None of those actions are in a category with what Elden might be up to!"

"Only a matter of degree!" she declared stoutly.

"Deliberate theft?" he grated.

"Well, maybe it is worse...."

"Much worse and you know it. Now let's think this through. What if Elden commissioned the film crew to try to shoot the book if they got the opportunity? They would have shot both strips of film at the same time, and they would have been mailing both strips to Santa Barbara. What if the film got into the wrong containers?"

"You mean Nick got my letters by mistake?"

"He could hardly admit it, could he? By asking to exchange the films he would be acknowledging his link with the military history in Molina's collection. A link which could prove very dangerous later on if the book was, indeed, stolen. Much simpler just to steal the film from you.''

"But there was no opportunity to do such a thing!" she protested desperately.

"The night of the party?" Jared offered a little too quietly. "He's been to your house before, presumably. He's probably even been in your study...?"

"Yes, but... Oh, my God!" What if Nick had done it? Alina told herself she didn't believe the accusations for a minute, but what if he had? Vittorio Molina was setting a trap which could eventually lead him to Nick....

"I'm not agreeing with your logic but just for the sake of argument, what would Molina do if he did catch s—someone like Nick in his little trap?" she asked distantly.

Again Jared hesitated. "Molina is a wealthy and powerful man. He could ruin Elden. Destroy his reputation with a few choice words in rare-book circles."

"Books are Nick's whole life! I've got to warn him. Pull over, Jared, I've got to find a phone...."

"You'll do nothing of the kind." Jared's hands tightened on the wheel, and the Ferrari seemed to pick up a bit more speed. "You're staying out of this, Alina."

"He's my partner," Alina raged, panicked and infuriated as she realized her helplessness. "I owe him this much, at least!"

"I thought you claimed he was innocent," Jared mocked. "If he is, nothing will come of Molina's trap."

"I'm going to warn him," she grated between her teeth.

"Why?"

"I've told you why! He's my friend and my partner. I owe him everything!"

"Is it more than friendship, Alina?" Jared rasped. "Or have you imagined yourself in love with your mentor all these years?"

"No!"

"I can see how it would happen," Jared went on with a touch of savagery. "You would idolize him as your teacher, be grateful to him for letting you buy into the business. He's got everything you thought you wanted in a lover, hasn't he? He's sophisticated, well educated, accepted in all the right academic circles...."

"Jared! Stop it!" Alina was horrified at the twist in the conversation.

"You're going to forget him, Alina. You belong to me now. I'm the one who came looking for you. Elden's waited too long to stake his claim...."

"Dammit! Stop talking as if I'm a piece of property! Can't you understand what I'm feeling toward

Nick? It's a question of loyalty to a man who's been a friend!'' Alina struggled to get control of herself and her voice. She was on the verge of hysteria as she realized Jared had no intention of letting her warn Nick. The knowledge that she might be unable to let her friend know what Molina was planning was so alarming that she knew she was starting to believe the accusations. But it didn't matter. Regardless of what Nick had done, she owed him the warning.

"Forget it, Alina," Jared advised coldly, as if he knew exactly what she was thinking.

"Jared, you have to believe me! I'm honor bound to warn him. I have an obligation to a friend...!''

Jared said nothing and Alina realized grimly he had no intention of arguing further. For the moment he was in control. She swallowed at the harshly etched planes of his face, reading there the strength of his determination.

"What about letting him know why I've disappeared?" she said a few minutes later, trying another tactic. "You said something about letting him think I've been swept off my feet?" she added tauntingly.

The green eyes flicked a brief, assessing glance at her carefully composed features. "In the morning you can phone him and tell him that you've eloped, and you'll be back at work after you've had a honeymoon."

"Are you crazy?" His unexpected suggestion destroyed Alina's composure at once. "What happens when I return after this fictitious honeymoon still single?"

"We can work out the details," he replied imperturbably.

"The details!" she yelped. "Jared Troy, are you by any chance proposing to me just to keep me from trying to warn Nick?" She glared at him, rather stunned.

"Not exactly. I'm proposing to you because we belong together. If you'll overlook a few of your intellectual prejudices and remember what we've shared, I think you'll realize that."

"You told me you weren't interested in marriage," Alina reminded him, her pulse leaping strangely in spite of the circumstances.

"That was shortly after you'd finished telling me what you thought of the institution, as I recall. I didn't want to scare you off completely at that early stage," he admitted easily, one shoulder lifting too casually.

"You...you mean you were thinking of marriage that first night when you showed up on my doorstep?" The words came out in a bare whisper.

"Somehow"—he grinned a bit dryly—"it seemed inevitable. What else can two people like us do? Correspond for the rest of our lives?"

Hardly the most romantic of proposals, Alina

thought sadly, subsiding into her seat as she tried vainly to sort out what was happening. Still, for a man like Jared to be offering marriage must mean he felt something of an abiding emotion toward her. Jared Troy was not the sort of man to talk of marriage if all he felt was a physical tie. Unwillingly she thought of the loneliness she'd read between the lines of his letters....

Abruptly she tore her mind away from such weakening thoughts. She had her obligation to Nick to think of first. Nick, the man who had made her career possible. The man who had given her such an important break, introduced her to so many crucial contacts in the rare-book world....

"Jared, whatever you and I may decide to do, I have to warn Nick."

"You're staying out of it, Alina," he returned evenly.

"I can't just sit by and take the risk...."

"The risk that he might be guilty?" Jared challenged.

"Yes, dammit!"

"I'll make you forget whatever you feel for him, Alina," he vowed. "Trust me."

"No, Jared. This time you have to trust me," Alina replied with unnatural calm as she acknowledged the truth of her own words. She turned to stare out the window at the blue Pacific again, her mind made up. She had no choice. Nick had to be warned.

"You're not going to do anything more on the telephone tomorrow morning than tell him you're getting married, Alina," Jared insisted.

"You can't stop me from warning him." Alina's head came around briefly to face him. She caught the enigmatic glance he tossed at her, and it sent a shiver down her spine. What had she gotten herself into when she'd begun the impassioned correspondence with Jared Troy? She should have known better than to fall in love with a dangerous, lonely *condottiere*, the kind of man who took what he wanted.

The remainder of the drive to Palm Springs passed in almost total silence. Alina felt edgy and uncertain of Jared's mood as he negotiated the maze of Los Angeles County freeways en route to the desert beyond. She didn't bring up the subject of Nick again, knowing with great certainty that he would still be violently opposed to any notion of her warning the other man. She could only wonder at the intensity of his feelings on the subject. It was as if a warning to Nick would constitute a betrayal of Jared.

It was the sight of the large, gleaming white house with its high-walled garden that broke Alina's self-imposed silence a long time later.

"It's like a private villa," she murmured, unable to resist the comparison.

"Like it?" Jared inquired a bit too casually as he brought the Ferrari to a halt in the circular drive.

"It's beautiful," Alina told him honestly as she studied the gardens and house through the high gate. "It's like something a Renaissance nobleman might have built in the country as a place to spend the summers."

The winding, palm-lined street continued on toward a distant golf course. Several other equally expensive residences were set well back from the curb at a discreet distance from each other. The brilliant sun had warmed the surrounding desert, and the mountains in the distance seemed purple in the bright light. Alina knew there would be a pool in the backyard of every elegant home.

"I got the basic design out of a treatise on Renaissance architecture," Jared said, reaching for the luggage as they climbed out of the Ferrari. "I had to make a few modifications, of course."

"You mean you didn't need dungeons or a banqueting hall?" she mocked, following as he led the way through the gate and into the cool, lush garden. A charming fountain which looked vaguely familiar formed a focal point. It took Alina a moment to realize that the familiarity was due to the fountain's style. It could have been cooling the garden of a wealthy citizen of fifteenth-century Florence.

The interior of the house with its high ceilings and

rich parquet flooring continued the overall effect of
an expensive, cool retreat. The furniture was low and
sleek with a masculine heaviness that fit very well
against the white walls. Floor to ceiling windows
opened out onto the shaded garden.

"Do you live here all alone?" Alina asked as
Jared set her suitcase down on the level above the
sunken living room.

"I have someone who comes in and cleans a couple of times a week and a gardener," he said, glancing at her. "Why?"

"Nothing. It's a lovely home. It just feels a little…" She broke off, not knowing how to put it into
words.

"A little empty?" he asked, his mouth quirking.

"Well, yes," she admitted.

"Why do you think I came looking for you?" he
asked simply. "Come on, I'll show you the rest of
the place."

She followed him through the house, glancing into
the large study with its sophisticated little computer
and shelves full of files and business books. The
kitchen was large and equipped with every conve-
nience, just as she expected. The master bedroom
was huge and beautifully furnished with a four-poster
bed. The windows along one wall also looked out
into the privacy of the garden. When Jared pointedly
set both suitcases down in that room near what ap-

peared to be an original of a Renaissance bridal chest, Alina tried to ignore the flicker of warmth in her veins. He was making it very clear where he felt she belonged.

But it was the library that captured her attention.

"Oh, Jared!" With a soft exclamation she hurried ahead of him into the panelled room lined with glass bookcases. In addition to the valuable books that filled the room, there were several exotic items of Renaissance military armor housed in a long case near the window. As she turned in a circle, not knowing where to start, the small reproduction of the *Gattamelata* statue caught her eye. The serenely grim face with its feeling of restrained and controlled power drew her toward the equestrian piece like a magnet. If there was something of Francesco in this little statue, there was something, too, of Jared.

"I could get lost in here," she said, running a hand lightly over the mounted figure and scanning the nearest bookcase with barely concealed hunger. The names of Machiavelli, Borgia, Medici, and Petrarch flashed in front of her eyes on the leather and cloth spines.

"That's not a bad idea," Jared said, watching her quietly from the doorway.

"Getting lost?" She spun around in surprise and then realized what he meant. Her mouth tightened and some of the excitement faded from her hazel eyes. "Oh. You mean so I won't be tempted to come out in time to warn Nick." Her tone turned abruptly flat.

"Let's not talk about him," Jared advised just as flatly.

"What would you rather talk about?"

"Dinner?" he suggested hopefully. She could almost feel the force of his will as he tried to draw a smile from her.

With a repressed sigh, Alina gave in for the moment. Nick had to be warned, but right now there really was no alternative except to eat. Besides, she was hungry.

They bustled around the huge kitchen, jointly fixing a salad, heating crusty French bread, and dropping the pasta into boiling water for fettuccine alfredo. There was a companionable atmosphere about the whole project which became an insidious attack on Alina's private decision to defy Jared. He looked so happy, she thought uneasily. He was really enjoying having someone to whom he could show off his beautiful home. And he liked sharing his kitchen with her.

Damn! she thought with self-disgust. How did a woman fight this kind of battle? She could sense Jared's desire for her, his decision to end the loneliness of his life by drawing her into his world, and she felt her love for him grow even as she remembered her obligation to Nick.

It was after dinner, which they ate at a round table near the window in the spacious kitchen, that Jared again brought up the subject of marriage. No topic could have been better calculated to make Alina's inner turmoil grow more chaotic.

"We can start the process tomorrow," he said calmly, pouring out the last of the wine.

"What process?" Alina asked, taken off guard.

"Getting married. It takes three days, you know. Unless you want to run over to Nevada?" he added agreeably, glancing up to meet her strained expression.

"Jared, are you sure this is what you want?" she managed, swallowing her wine in a rather large gulp.

"I'm sure." The green eyes glittered across the table at her. "You will marry me, won't you, Alina? We're right for each other. I know it with more certainty than I've ever known anything in my life."

"There are so many things to be considered," she began helplessly.

"If Elden was going to marry you, he would have done so long before I came on the scene!" Jared interrupted with sudden harshness.

"Nick and I have never been lovers!"

"And you never will be. Not now." He reached out to catch her nervously moving hand and hold it tightly in his own, his eyes boring into hers with an unnerving combination of pleading and determination. "Marry me, Alina. This week."

The world seemed to be turning a little too fast. Alina knew there were things that had to be said, important matters which should have been discussed. And there was the problem of warning Nick....

But the emerald eyes were capturing her, weaving their spell around her until she could think of nothing else in that moment except her love for Jared. She loved the man and he had just asked her to marry him. And she could trust him. Above all, she was certain of that. Jared would never cheat on her with another woman. He would never have asked her to marry him if he didn't intend to honor the commitment with the full force of his strong nature. In time, he would learn that what he felt for her was love....

"Yes, Jared. I'll marry you."

He was on his feet, coming around the small table to pull her up into his arms with a passionate need that was composed of far more than sheer male desire. "Alina, my lovely Alina. I swear you won't be sorry," he said huskily against her hair, his hands moving down her back to draw her tightly against him.

"Jared," she ventured unevenly, her love for him making it almost impossible to bring up the subject he kept rejecting. "There's still the problem of the film...."

"Forget it. It's not our problem any longer," he grated, sweeping her up into his arms. "Tonight we've got better things to do."

"Such as?" she asked with a flash of humor as he began striding down the wide hall to his bedroom.

"Such as celebrating our marriage," he declared with a dagger smile.

"Ah, but we aren't quite married yet," she pointed out, already succumbing to the tug of his desire.

"I think we were married five hundred years ago," he answered equably, using the toe of his shoe to push open the door of the bedroom. "We're just going to give California the courtesy of respecting its laws."

"You think Francesco and Battista were eventually married?" Alina lifted her arms to circle his neck as he slid her gently to her feet beside the bed.

"Naturally. What else could they have done? They were caught in the same situation we are. A man and a woman who need each other, want each other..."

Love each other? Alina finished silently as his passion began making itself felt in the tautening lines of his body.

"And understand each other," Jared concluded, burying his lips beneath the fall of bronzed brown

hair he had taken down with a quick movement of
his fingers.

Swiftly, tenderly, he removed her clothes, leaving
them in a pool at her feet. Alina moaned softly as
his hands traveled over her nakedness, delighting in
the texture of her skin, seeking the sensitive places
with unerring accuracy.

"Jared." She sighed, leaning into his strength and
letting it stir the desire in her. Tentatively and then
with growing certainty, she helped him undress.

Jared's urgency seemed at a new high tonight, she
realized as the excitement in him fed her own
aroused emotions. It was as if he needed to be sure
of her yet again, as if he would use his body to re-
inforce the claim he had made verbally.

He caught the smooth flesh of her rounded buttocks, pressing her against his lean thighs with a muttered groan. Then he lifted her briefly once more,
settling her onto the sheets and coming down beside
her with a possessiveness that told its own tale.

Alina felt her skin burn wherever his lips and
hands touched her, searing the nipples of her breasts,
branding the insides of her thighs, heating the softness of her stomach. She simmered beneath his urgent, demanding touch, her fingers playing along the
hardness of his body, digging into the muscled flesh
with feminine command.

"I want to be the only one who can make you

come alive like this," he rasped against her shoulder, his teeth gently tormenting her sensitized flesh. "Tell me there won't be anyone else, Alina. I think I would go mad if you were ever to want another man!"

"There is no one else, Jared," she whispered huskily, twisting languidly beneath his touch. "There has never been anyone who could do this to me. I would never leave you for anyone else!"

It was nothing less than the truth, she thought, and then she stopped thinking altogether as he parted her legs with his own, covering her softness completely even as she enveloped his strength.

Ten

Alina's conscience forced reality back upon her before she even opened her eyes to the desert sunrise the next morning. Nothing had changed. Her dilemma remained.

Beside her Jared lay in a glorious sprawl of lean, tanned skin and tangled white sheets. The dark lashes lay along the high cheekbones, softening the severe lines of his face. Alina turned her head on the pillow for a moment to look at him with love and a tenderness she hadn't known it was possible to feel for a man. Then, reluctantly, she slid out of the wide bed.

Finding a short toweling robe in the huge closet, she belted it around her waist and padded soundlessly across the tapestrylike area rug that covered the parquet flooring in front of the bed. Coming to a halt in front of the window she stood gazing unseeingly into the garden.

A beautiful home but with a strange loneliness about it that disturbed her. No she took that back. It wasn't precisely loneliness she sensed, but a self-imposed isolation. She had the impression that Jared simply hadn't felt the need of other people for a long time. Not until he had started reading between the lines of her letters and had begun constructing a fantasy of a woman who could play Battista to his Francesco? But he didn't treat her like a fantasy woman. A part of her felt safe in the knowledge that Jared saw her as herself, regardless of what might have led him to her in the first place.

She heard him stir behind her and then his voice came, a little husky still from sleep and remembered passion.

"Come back to bed, sweetheart. We're on our honeymoon."

Alina nerved herself for what must come next.

"No, Jared. The honeymoon comes after the marriage. And you may not want to marry me when this is over." She didn't look at him. She couldn't. It was tearing her apart to deliver the ultimatum, but she had no choice.

The silence from the bed told her he had understood her meaning. Tensely she awaited his fury, her arms folded protectively in front of her.

But it wasn't anger she sensed lapping at her as the silence deepened. It was something infinitely more devastating. It was despair.

"You can't get him out of your head, can you?" Jared finally said with a terrible resignation. "No matter what you feel when you're with me, lying in my arms, he still comes first, doesn't he?"

"Jared..." Her voice was a broken thread as she tried to find the words to combat his accusation.

"I told myself last night when you agreed to marry me that you must be putting Elden behind you. But it isn't that, is it? You've realized he's probably never going to return your love, so you're willing to accept my proposal instead."

She heard the self-torture in his words and shivered. The bed made a soft sound as Jared levered himself to his elbow. She could feel his eyes burning into her back. "Jared, will you please listen to me? Trust me? What I have to do is out of a sense of loyalty to a friend...."

"You're not going to him, Alina." She heard the steel in him, felt it subduing the despair as his will once again dominated his emotions. "You're mine and one of these days, one of these nights, you'll realize it. There's no future for you with a man like

Elden. Can't you understand that? He's not worth your love, dammit!''

A searing exasperation that was part anger and part disgust with the obtuseness of the male of the species abruptly gripped Alina. She turned around, her hair swinging softly across her shoulders, her hazel eyes alight with furious gold.

''You idiot!'' she nearly yelled. ''I'm not in love with Nicholas Elden! I have never been in love with Nicholas Elden or anyone else for that matter! I wasn't even truly in love with my ex-husband! It took a thick-headed, stubborn, arrogant, domineering *condottiere* of a man to teach me what love is all about. Everything I've ever felt for anyone else could only at best be labeled affection. It's you I love, Jared Troy! Heaven knows why! I've always had a preference for *intelligent* men, not mule-brained, one-track thinkers who can't seem to comprehend the success of their own seduction techniques!''

''Alina!''

He was sitting straight up in bed now, his eyes locked to hers. The emerald depths were blazing to life with a wonder and hope which should have slowed down her tirade but didn't. She was too wound up now to quit.

''Furthermore, if this is the sort of male obstinacy poor Battista had to put up with, I can certainly understand her decision not to let Francesco back into the villa! There is nothing more annoying than a man who doesn't recognize a woman's love when she's handing it to him on a silver platter.''

Jared was swinging his legs over the edge of the bed, utterly unconcerned with his own magnificent nakedness as he started toward her. "Alina, my sweet vixen, you can yell at me all you want. Just tell me it's true. Tell me you really do love me!''

"Of course I love you! Do you think I'd let myself be dragged off by a bullying, intimidating, annoying man like you if I didn't love you? Do you think I'd have taken your word alone about the missing microfilm if I didn't love you? Do you think I would—''

She never got a chance to utter the last of her rhetorical questions as Jared reached her, pulling her into his arms and successfully stopping the flow of words with his lips.

At his touch, Alina subsided, allowing herself to lean against his bare chest. He absorbed her weight as if it were nothing, his kiss deepening until he was drinking from her mouth as if he had been suffering from a thirst only she could satisfy.

"Alina, Alina," he finally managed in a slightly drugged voice. "I'd hoped and prayed and wanted so badly. I was afraid to let myself believe it might be true. I was going to give you time. I told myself that with time you'd realize the attraction between us was more than physical...."

"Oh, lord," she muttered against his shoulder in renewed disgust. "The ego of a man. You thought I've been going to bed with you just because you're such a fantastic lover?"

She felt the sudden warmth in his skin and realized he was flushing. The knowledge delighted her. She giggled softly, tightening her arms around his waist. Then she relented.

Lifting her head, she met his eyes with teasing humor in her own. "Oh, Jared. You are a fantastic lover. But that's not why I've been willing to share your bed. I'm not even sure I knew the whole reason myself until a short time ago. I guess the idea of loving you grew so naturally with the flow of our letters that I never even knew what had happened to me until you walked into my life in person!"

"And I've loved you since that first nasty little letter you wrote to the editor of that journal in response to the article I'd written," he confessed with hoarse honesty. "When you opened your door to me the night of the party, I wanted to pick you up and carry you off right then and there. I realized that whatever I'd been feeling toward the woman who wrote those letters, it was nothing compared to the feelings I had when I finally met her face to face."

"You love me, Jared?" Alina murmured, her face glowing with happiness.

"With all my heart and soul. I've never needed a woman the way I need you. I've never wanted one the way I want you. It's as if you're a part of me. A part I've been subconsciously searching for all my life. You don't know what you're doing to me by telling me that you're in love, too. I feel as if the world suddenly became complete. Oh, God, Alina...!"

As if he'd run out of words to express the intensity of his emotions, Jared folded her back into his arms, his kiss a passionate, tender, deeply moving caress which made the world spin. In that moment, Alina knew the sensation would last a lifetime. Perhaps longer.

"Speaking of stupidity," Jared finally mumbled against her mouth, "you can share the prize with me! A woman like you, a self-admitted, accomplished tease, should have known when a man was totally stricken!"

"Not when that man is so different from any other she has ever known," Alina defended herself blissfully. "I wasn't sure *condottieri* really understood love...."

"That's probably why you never understood Francesco," he retorted knowledgeably.

"Hah!"

"Calm down, we'll get back to that argument soon enough. This is our time, not Battista's and Francesco's!" Jared grinned. Then he sobered. "But I think, perhaps, neither of us fully understood love, hmmm?"

"Perhaps," she admitted. "And perhaps neither of us really understood exactly what was missing in our lives. I'd filled mine with my career, my parties, my superficial friends...."

"And I'd filled mine with business and book collecting. I figured I'd given marriage a chance...."

"So had I. We both picked mates who fit our requirements at the time, I think," Alina said slowly, remembering how Jared had once spoken of his "business" marriage.

"But the requirements we'd established were all wrong," Jared concluded softly, with deep conviction.

"Yes." For a long time Alina simply stood in the circle of his arms, content. She sensed the same contentment welling up in Jared, and it brought her a happiness she would not have believed possible.

It was Jared who finally broke the gentle moment.

"It's all right now, Alina," he finally said on a long sigh which drained away all the tension in his body.

She raised her head to stare at him mutely, knowing what he meant.

"Go ahead, if you feel you owe it to him," he went on quietly. "I don't think he deserves the warning, but I can understand your feeling that you have to do something. And maybe, just maybe, he's not guilty, anyway," he added magnanimously.

"You trust me? Trust my love for you?" she asked softly.

"I trust you. You couldn't look at me like that, tell me you love me and be lying," he stated with great certainty. Then he groaned ruefully. "Now that I know for sure that you love me, you'll probably be able to wrap me around your little finger!"

"What a pleasant thought." Alina grinned, looking entranced at the notion. Then her smile faded and she caught his face between his palms, standing on tiptoe to brush her mouth lightly against his. "Thank you, Jared."

She made the call a few hours later. Jared chose to disappear into his study, and Alina knew the action was prompted by a general conviction that Nick didn't deserve a warning rather than a failure to understand her motives.

By the time she replaced the receiver, however, she was in a state of shock. Too stunned to go in search of Jared, Alina wandered out into the garden and sat down on the white rock edge of the sparkling fountain.

Jared found her there and crossed the lawn with

an expression of concern on his face as he took in her strange, quiet air. "What is it, honey?" he asked gently, sitting down beside her. "Do you feel sorry for him?"

Alina lifted her head to meet his eyes, her hand trailing absently in the fountain of water. "It's incredible, Jared. Absolutely incredible." She shook her head disbelievingly. "To work so long with someone and never really know him. When I confronted him as gently as I could with the situation and Molina's name, Nick just sort of...gave up. He told me the whole story...."

"Including why?"

"He gambles," she said simply, still struck by the fact that she had never guessed Nick's secret. "I had no idea. No one I know would have guessed it. But it explains why I always had the feeling he became a different person when he wasn't around the shop or at a party. A friend of mine thought he was gay and ashamed of it, but she was way off base. I've heard of people who get themselves involved in heavy gambling debts but I've never known one.... At least I assumed I didn't know one!"

"So he needed money on occasion down through the years? A lot of it at times?" Jared hazarded with a knowing tone in his deep voice.

"Yes."

"And the obvious way for him to get it was in the profession he knew best."

"I'm afraid so. I don't think there were very many such instances. One time, I myself came to the rescue and saved him from having to resort to theft!" Her mouth twisted wryly as she remembered that part of the conversation with Nick.

"The time he 'let' you buy into partnership with him?"

Alina nodded, no longer surprised by Jared's guessing. He seemed to have a better understanding of some aspects of human nature than she did!

"Did he explain about the theft of the microfilm?"

"He took it the night of the party. The day before, he had discovered that there had been a mix-up. The head of the film crew had phoned him in a panic and explained that I had been sent the wrong film. Nick knows my study and it was a simple enough matter for him to search the desk during the party. He panicked, didn't think to substitute my film for the one he was taking. But he figured there was nothing to throw suspicion on him. He didn't realize that I'd made a copy or that you would be around to recognize the significance of the crew's filming that particular book."

"You told him about me?" Jared demanded thoughtfully.

"I had to."

"It's all right. I'm glad you made it quite clear you're not the only one who knows what's going on," he told her deliberately.

Alina blinked. "Surely you don't think Nick would try to...try to do something to me!"

"Not now. Not with Molina and I both knowing the score," Jared assured her with a measure of satisfaction.

Alina brushed such thoughts aside. Nick would never hurt her. He had been a pitiful case on the phone. They had been friends long enough that he knew she would never use any information against him. But there was another matter to be considered now. How could she continue to work side by side with Nick Elden? She pushed that thought to the back of her mind, too.

"What will Molina do?" she asked instead.

Jared shrugged. "Nothing. He has no proof and he wouldn't act without it. You can rest assured he'll keep an eye on Elden's activities in the future, however! Maybe that alone will be enough to make your partner behave himself!"

Alina repressed a shiver. Would it? Gamblers were notorious for resorting to desperate efforts to recover their losses. And she was the man's partner! No, came the clear thought. She couldn't remain in business with Nick Elden. She would never be able to trust the man again, and he was too likely to use their friendship, assuming she would help him out if he got into trouble in the future. She had to get out.

She knew Jared was watching the play of thoughts across her features, but he didn't question her on them. Instead he got to his feet with an easy movement, the quick, dagger grin lighting his face.

"Come on. It's over and I have a much better method of enjoying what's left of the morning before we go out and apply for the wedding license!"

Alina narrowed her eyes with mocking suspicion as she allowed herself to be tugged to her feet. "You're insatiable!" she accused.

He gave her a reproachful glance, taking hold of her wrist and guiding her through the garden. "I assure you I have nothing more seductive in mind than a little morning exercise!"

"Uh-huh... Oh! We're going for a swim?" She tossed him a laughing glance as he drew her to a halt by the pool. "I'll go and get my suit...."

"Unnecessary. We have all the privacy in the world here," he assured her, his fingers going to the buttons of her striped shirt.

"Jared!" A little shocked, in spite of her California attitude toward such things, Alina made a half-laughing attempt to fend him off. She stepped backward, just out of reach and clutched her shirtfront.

"Don't tell me you're going to revert to the teasing games again," he groaned, a devil leaping to life in the emerald eyes as he closed the distance between them.

"It's just that I'll feel comfortable in a suit," she explained quickly, sensing his intent. She held up a hand, warding him off. "Now, Jared, I'm serious...."

"So am I," he murmured deeply, snagging her around the waist and tugging her close to lift her lightly into his arms. "You and Battista may have made careers out of teasing men, but both of you should know by now that Francesco and I are exceptions. We don't allow too much of that sort of thing."

Before she could hastily agree to undress, Jared walked to the edge of the pool.

"Jared! Wait, I'll—"

Her shriek was cut off as he stepped, fully clothed, into the pool, still holding her in his arms. The crystal water closed over both their heads, and Alina floundered under the surface for a long moment before finding her way to the top.

"Damn *condottiere!*" she hissed, flicking the wet hair off her face with a toss of her head. She glared at him as he surfaced beside her, laughing.

She wanted to go on berating him, but in that moment she suddenly realized the deep happiness in him. A happiness which had not been there the night she had first opened her door to the *condottiere* waiting at the villa gate. And she was the cause of that happiness, Alina realized with womanly wisdom and pleasure. He loved her, just as much as she loved him. Instead of yelling at him, she submitted to his touch with delicious satisfaction as he swam toward her and began peeling off her wet clothes.

In a few moments both pairs of jeans had been heaved, soaking wet, up onto the pool's edge, along with the remainder of their garments. The laughter faded in their eyes as passion rose to take its place.

"I was wondering," Jared whispered as little huskily as his hands slid over her body, "how you might feel about a new partnership?"

Alina floated in the water, letting him support her near-weightlessness with strong hands which circled her waist. "I've already agreed to marry you," she reminded him, eyes half closed.

He shook his head. "I'm not talking about marriage. We'll be married, all right, but marriage isn't a partnership, sweetheart!"

She arched one eyebrow and then decided to argue that one with him later. "You're referring to a *business* partnership?"

He inserted one hair-roughened thigh between her legs, easing her against him with erotic deliberation that sent shivers of expectation down her spine. "I thought you might be in the market for one," he said meaningfully. "You must realize you can't stay with Elden now."

Alina's eyes snapped open. "How did you know I'd started worrying about that?"

"It's obvious, honey." he said gently. "What were you thinking of doing?"

She hesitated. "Perhaps going into business for myself."

"Corey Books?"

"Has a nice ring, don't you think?" she asked saucily.

"I like the sound of Corey and Troy better." He grinned. "Think of the contacts we'd have between the two of us!"

"I thought you enjoyed playing the wolf of Wall Street," Alina temporized, her mind going to work on the idea of a business partnership with her future husband.

"I told you once, it's been a practical way to pay for my real interest, which is book collecting. I wouldn't have to give it up completely. I could always go back to it if we needed fresh capital."

"Corey and Troy, hmmm?" Alina mused, the warm humor flaring in her eyes.

"Interested?" He grinned, sweeping her closer against his naked chest.

"I could be persuaded."

"I have a little something extra with which to sweeten the deal," he murmured coaxingly, beginning to nibble gently on her earlobe.

"What's that?"

"The wedding gift I'm going to persuade Vittorio Molina to give us," he drawled invitingly.

"Another copy of those letters?" Alina pulled back from the deepening embrace, excitement momentarily pushing aside the passion. "Really, Jared? You can persuade him to refilm them?"

"I'll want your signature on the dotted line, first, naturally." He chuckled. "And Vittorio will want another agency to do the filming!"

"I'll sign! I'll sign!" Alina agreed enthusiastically. "And Molina can choose any agency he wants! Speaking of which, however..."

"What's he going to do with the crooked film crew? I don't know. I'll have to talk to him. My guess is, he'll simply put out the word that they're not to be trusted. It won't take long for them to stop getting the juicier assignments. There's probably no way of proving anything against them."

"I hope Nick meant what he said on the phone." Alina sighed, remembering her soon-to-be-ex-partner's words.

"Made a promise to quit gambling, I suppose?"

"You don't sound as if you believe he will?"

"Let's say I have my doubts. It's not easy to fight that kind of compulsion. But now he knows that Molina's on to him, he may find other ways of covering his debts! About compulsions, however. I have one, too...." He wrapped his arms around her, pulling her close until the hair of his chest teased her nipples.

Alina twisted happily, her legs tangling with his. "I love you so much, Jared!"

"You couldn't love me any more than I love you, he rasped, his body responding to hers with unmistakable need. "When I think of all the times I reread your letters, imagining what I'd do if I had you there beside me in person...!" He finished the sentence on an urgent groan.

Alina felt him fall effortlessly backward through the water until he was sitting on the pool steps. He settled her eager body along the length of his, taking possession of it as he took possession of her mouth.

They made love with a grace induced by the watery environment, slowly, lingeringly, lovingly. Jared watched through passion-slitted eyes as the final moment came for her. Alina arched thrillingly, her ecstatic cry caught in her throat. As she was woman enough to know that the sight of her responding to him had a devastatingly erotic effect on Jared. His own muffled shout soon followed as he surged powerfully upward, holding her so tightly she had to gulp for breath.

Down, down they came, literally and figuratively, each lost in their very private world, clinging to each other until they suddenly found themselves trying to breathe water.

The shock brought them floundering, laughing, to the surface, still holding each other tightly, the loving mystery of the moment still showing in their eyes.

"This particular technique may take a little practice," Jared admitted with a grin, catching his breath. "We'll work on it after we get the license. Which reminds me, it's about time we got going on that project...."

"I wonder if Francesco tried to rush Battista into marriage when he returned," Alina mused as Jared glided back toward the steps, one hand around her waist.

"No doubt about it. It's the only way to cure a professional tease," Jared declared, hauling her up to the edge of the pool. "Nothing like marriage to the right men to settle down women like you and Battista!"

"Who would have thought," Alina began as she lifted her face for his kiss, "that a couple of *condottieri* would know so much about women!"

"Only about two very special women," Jared whispered against her lips, "just two very, very special women. Francesco got his Battista and now, after all this time, I've got my Alina."

He sealed the claim with his kiss.

* * * * *

SPECIAL EDITION

Stories of love and life, these powerful
novels are tales that you can identify with—
romances with "something special" added
in!

Fall in love with the stories of authors such
as **Nora Roberts, Diana Palmer, Ginna Gray**
and many more of your special favorites—as
well as wonderful new voices!

Special Edition brings you
entertainment for the heart!

SILHOUETTE®

Desire®

Do you want...

Dangerously handsome heroes

Evocative, everlasting love stories

Sizzling and tantalizing sensuality

Incredibly sexy miniseries like **MAN OF THE MONTH**

Red-hot romance

Enticing entertainment that can't be beat!

You'll find all of this, and much *more* each and every month in **SILHOUETTE DESIRE**. Don't miss these unforgettable love stories by some of romance's hottest authors. Silhouette Desire—where your fantasies will always come true....

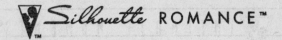
Silhouette ROMANCE™

What's a single dad to do when he needs a wife by next Thursday?

Who's a confirmed bachelor to call when he finds a baby on his doorstep?

How does a plain Jane in love with her gorgeous boss get him to notice her?

From classic love stories to romantic comedies to emotional heart tuggers, **Silhouette Romance** offers six irresistible novels every month by some of your favorite authors! Such as...beloved bestsellers **Diana Palmer, Annette Broadrick, Suzanne Carey, Elizabeth August** and **Marie Ferrarella**, to name just a few—and some sure to become favorites!

Fabulous Fathers...Bundles of Joy...Miniseries... Months of blushing brides and convenient weddings... Holiday celebrations... You'll find all this and much more in **Silhouette Romance**—always emotional, always enjoyable, always about love!

WAYS TO UNEXPECTEDLY MEET MR. RIGHT:

♡ Go out with the sexy-sounding stranger your daughter secretly set you up with through a personal ad.

♡ RSVP yes to a wedding invitation—soon it might be your turn to say "I do!"

♡ Receive a marriage proposal by mail— from a man you've never met.....

These are just a few of the unexpected ways that written communication leads to love in Silhouette Yours Truly.

Each month, look for two fast-paced, fun and flirtatious Yours Truly novels (with entertaining treats and sneak previews in the back pages) by some of your favorite authors—and some who are sure to become favorites.

YOURS TRULY™:
Love—when you least expect it!

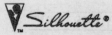

Silhouette®

FIVE UNIQUE SERIES
FOR EVERY WOMAN YOU ARE...

❦ Silhouette ROMANCE™

From classic love stories to romantic comedies to emotional heart tuggers, Silhouette Romance is sometimes sweet, sometimes sassy—and always enjoyable! Romance—the way you always knew it could be.

SILHOUETTE® Desire®

Red-hot is what we've got! Sparkling, scintillating, *sensuous* love stories. Once you pick up one you won't be able to put it down...only in Silhouette Desire.

Silhouette® SPECIAL EDITION®

Stories of love and life, these powerful novels are tales that you can identify with—romances with "something special" added in! Silhouette Special Edition is entertainment for the heart.

SILHOUETTE·INTIMATE·MOMENTS®

Enter a world where passions run hot and excitement is always high. Dramatic, larger than life and always compelling—Silhouette Intimate Moments provides captivating romance to cherish forever.

❦ SILHOUETTE YOURS TRULY™

A personal ad, a "Dear John" letter, a wedding invitation... Just a few of the ways that written communication unexpectedly leads Miss Unmarried to Mr. "I Do" in Yours Truly novels...in the most fun, fast-paced and flirtatious style!